CLOSE ENOUGH
TO KILL

CLOSE ENOUGH
TO KILL

•

Marjorie M. McGinley

AVALON BOOKS
NEW YORK

PRINTED IN THE UNITED STATES OF AMERICA
ON ACID-FREE PAPER
BY HADDON CRAFTSMEN, BLOOMSBURG, PENNSYLVANIA

To all my friends; you know who you are.

Chapter One

It was said of Faith Christine Butler that she could out-argue a Supreme Court judge, a couple of two-year-old kids, and three mules all at the same time.

This was not without a grain of truth in it because every-one knew her brother was a State Supreme Court judge, she had young grandchildren, and three large, notoriously independent, and stubborn sons . . . besides her mules.

She was a large-boned woman and wide and flat of body; there was nothing fat or frivolous about her. Her clothing consisted of black or navy T-shirts that she got at Harvey's Discount Store (seconds) and good, sturdy, well-worked-in black or blue Levi jeans.

Her graying hair was pulled back in a functional pony tail with an elastic.

Because of the mules—they tended to step on your

1

feet—she wore rugged leather cowboy boots instead of sneakers.

You might have wanted to stick your nose up at Faith Christine, but she had earned the respect of people—some grudgingly—in spite of her dress habits.

This was because she was the person to call in our small community of Rushing River Junction in Northern California if things went wrong in your life.

She would help if she could. She was unexpectedly helpful in ways that most of us could only imagine because of the strange pull she had on people of all walks of life. This strange assortment had one thing in common: they could all see something valuable and rare in Faith Christine.

So it wasn't unusual that July morning to see a snub-nosed, thin man of medium height, in an impeccably tailored dark black suit, talking to Faith Christine. They were standing, deeply engrossed in talk, in front of the open door of her mule barn.

I arrived before noon with some homegrown carrots that I had just pulled and washed. I figured he was one of her many friends, come for some advice. I sat in my blue Ford truck at a respectful distance, and waited my turn.

Then Faith nodded almost imperceptibly at me that I was doing the right thing waiting in my truck, so I knew a few things. One, he was not there on a friendly visit, and two, he was not someone I wanted any contact with, or she would have called me over and introduced me in the friendly way country people have with people who have their seal of approval. In other words, he was trouble.

He left, and she came over as I got out of my truck. She didn't give me any of her usual guff about my carrots; she usually pretended she hated them and then ate every one for supper that night. Sometimes, we ate them together.

I had begun bringing her vegetables from my garden the year her husband and my wife died. Mine, of cancer, her husband on a business trip in a 37-vehicle fog-caused pileup a hundred miles south of here. Her husband Henry had been killed three months before Dora died, and Faith Christine kindly helped me with the funeral and afterward, with my grief, in May of that same year. We had that in common—our grief. That was three years ago.

We had more in common; all our children were grown and left, and we each lived alone. Now I could see she was upset. I didn't ask what the trouble was. She would have told me right off if she was planning to. None of my business, obviously. Anyway, asking questions was not the way to get information around here, a holdover from the old days of the West, here in Northern California. The way to get information was to talk about other things, until the other person was ready to either discuss it, or not. I talked about my garden, my cattle, my fruit trees, and about the weather. She nodded from time to time in a distracted way. Shortly, I was talked out, and I was getting ready to leave when she looked up at me with inquiring eyes, gauging whether or not she should tell me her troubles. I knew it was a tough decision, as she was a proud woman.

Our eyes held, and I did not waver. I could see her mind leaping ahead, deciding what to say. Her lips had dried from anxiety. They were usually soft and full.

"You know," I said, "I set a lot of store by you." That was an old-fashioned expression we had both jokingly used in the past that meant we held each other in high regard.

She was standing stiffly silent. This was so unlike Faith

Christine. I was silent, too, and took a long look at her house, barn, corral, and outbuildings; all looked in order, the same as always. No clue there.

"Mules all right?" I asked.

She nodded yes.

"Kids?"

Again she nodded yes.

"Grandkids?"

"Fine."

The sudden sadness of her look threw me off balance.

I looked intensely at her, and this time her brown eyes dropped quickly, also looking at the ground. I wanted to help if I could.

She turned and looked toward Gray Mist Mountain, which both our properties bordered. The spectacular mountain view was one reason Dora and I had bought our land here twenty years ago.

Faith Christine made her living renting out her mules— complete with picks, shovels, mining pans, and all the other prospecting equipment a person needed. People came from just about everywhere to try their luck for a day or a week or a month, prospecting on the public land on Gray Mist Mountain. It was a relatively safe mountain, and people were able to fulfill, in some cases, a lifelong dream.

Before anyone left, they had to listen to a lecture from Faith Christine on the care of her mules. The mules, in fact, knew the way so well that they were a free guide for novice prospectors. Some of Faith Christine's customers had been coming for years. There was an ancient dry creek bed that ran upward for many miles that prospectors loved. An earthquake had changed the path of a river in ancient times.

With picks, axes, and sometimes homemade sluices, the

prospectors dug under boulders, in crevices, in dry stream beds, and panned in the clear cold streams on Gray Mist.

Sometimes they found flakes or grains of gold, sometimes not; most didn't care. It was the hunt that was thrilling in itself. In the last few years, Faith Christine had had a little booklet printed up with safety and useful tips, as well as mule care information. We both felt a kinship with the kind of people who chose prospecting for a vacation.

I decided to try a bit of mule philosophy on Faith Christine. Whenever a mule's being stubborn and won't go forward, just pretend you want him to go backward, and pull him backward with the lead. Being a cussed stubborn creature, he will then go forward.

"Well, I'd best be going then," I said, bluffing. I made a fake move to leave. It worked.

"No, wait, John," she said, looking steadily up at me. "That man that was here? He's a lawyer. He says the government's going to close Gray Mist to prospectors."

"That would be a foolish move. That mountain gives a lot of innocent pleasure to a lot of people," I said, feeling the heat of anger rise within me. "It's public land."

Somehow I knew by the way she was still holding her breath that there was more. I felt myself scowling.

"What else?"

"After it's closed, the government is going to lease the mineral mining rights to a Canadian company."

"For a couple of dollars an acre, as usual?"

She nodded, crying. It was a sight that was very unfamiliar in the many years I had known her, and very disconcerting. I patted her shoulder awkwardly.

"We'll have to fight it, Faith Christine," I said.

"We can't," she said. "We're both just 'little people.' "

"Don't be too sure about that," I said.

"I'm too old to be fighting a war as big as this," Faith Christine said.

Using her own terminology, I said, "That's mule muck." I smiled at her. She didn't smile back. We walked to her house to sit on the chairs on her porch. She went to take the old rocking chair, but that was too symbolic so I shot over there ahead of her, cut her off at the pass, so to speak, and sat down.

She looked a little surprised at that; it was unlike me, but this called for unusual measures. I was already sure of that. She sat on one of the straightback chairs. Finally I said, "It's wrong, you know, what they're doing. I have a high regard for the Canadian people but it is not the good Canadian people themselves who are doing this. It's outsiders taking advantage of our laws. Our government has a responsibility not to give away mineral rights that are a national resource—that belong to the American people— to another nation. It's just plumb wrong. Funny we didn't hear anything about this before now."

"What can we do about it?" she said.

"First, let's see if we can find out the exact people behind this. We need names, Faith Christine. That will be your first job."

"What are you going to do?" she asked.

"Me?" I said, rising and circling the house so that I could get a look at Gray Mist Mountain. I knew they used great big machines to chew up rock to extract gold, leaving cyanide, toxic wastes, and desolation to land and water. Faith Christine followed me and we looked in silence, picturing enormous yellow bulldozers and blasters on the beautiful rugged mountain behind our homes.

"They'll come in from this side," I said, "because the other side of the mountain is sheer cliff. This isn't too different, in principle, from a range war. Only this time it's a mountain range."

"You gave me *my* assignment, General; what are *you* going to do?" Faith Christine said. "Or should I call you John Wayne instead of General?" I ignored that.

"Me?" I repeated. "I'm going to think."

Chapter Two

The next time I saw Faith Christine, I was in for a big surprise. My mouth dropped open like an orphan calf waiting for the bottle, as she came out of the door of her house.

Her hair was its original shade of golden brown—the one that I remembered from years ago. It was cut short around her face, and softly curled. She had on a navy blue businesswoman's suit complete with classy white blouse, stockings, and high heels.

She had makeup on. In fact, I hardly recognized her.

She looked pleased at my expression. She looked like a city businesswoman.

"Where's Faith Christine?" I asked politely. "I'd like to speak to her if possible."

She caught on quickly. "I'm not sure," she said. "I'll see if she's available."

"Faith Christine," I said, "you sure look great, but what's going on?"

"Well, you said we're fighting a range war, like in the old days. I decided when you walk among the enemy, you better have the same uniform on. So, I did what is another old western tradition: I reinvented myself."

"You sure did," I said admiringly.

"It's big gossip in town," she said. "I'm surprised you didn't hear about it."

"I haven't been to town much," I said. "I've been on the ranch, thinking." I was still in shock, and I admit it, a little awed looking at her. She looked very pretty.

"How did you make out?" I said.

"At first," she said, "not very well. Tuesday I went to the State Capitol building looking the way I usually did and they pretended I didn't exist. I was invisible . . . a nobody. I couldn't even get an appointment and nobody would talk to me."

I nodded. "Let's go inside," she said. "These shoes are killing me." I was still fascinated by her hair. We went in, straight through the living room and to the back of the house. We sat at her pine trestle table in the kitchen, near the big picture window. I gazed for a moment out the window at the beautiful point of the old mountain. Indians here say Gray Mist has a spirit, or soul. I don't know about that, but I do know it has beauty. And that's worth something, as much as a work of art that people love.

I sighed. I looked back at Faith Christine.

I was still amazed at her hair. I wanted to reach over and touch it. Two beauties. The mountain and her.

"Your hair sure looks pretty, Faith Christine," I said.

"Here," she said, leaning over the table at me. "Touch it, feel how soft it is." I did. It was.

"It's a long time since I spent any money on myself," she said. "Permanents have improved."

So have you, I wanted to say, but the words caught in my throat. Not that I didn't like the old Faith Christine— far from it. But this one—her reinventing—made my heart beat faster. I felt like a fool. *I'm as bad as the others,* I thought, judging by outward appearances. *John Richard Ranger, you're an old fool.*

"I'm glad you did," I said truthfully. I coughed to hide my feelings. "So, on with your story," I said.

"Where were we?" she said.

"Getting nowhere dressed as your old self," I said, wondering if I was saying one of those things men say that inexplicably make a woman furious at you so that they don't talk to you for days and days.

She didn't seem to notice. "Well, my new self marched right in there and began forcefully demanding answers. I wasn't rude, but I drew myself up to my tallest height, and tried to look imposing." I could picture that. "And," she said dramatically, "it worked. Or, at least, it seems to be working. I got people angry at the injustice of the Feds allowing our mountain to be destroyed."

"The Feds?" I said. "You're talkin' like a TV show cop." She knew I was teasing.

"Anyway, I didn't know it, but an Indian group is already protesting in Washington, as are a couple of other environmental groups who got wind of it . . . and you are right, they *were* trying to sneak it through as quietly as possible. And . . ." She paused dramatically. "I'm going to be on TV tomorrow, to talk about it on the six o'clock news. They are going to do an interview. I'm going to mention the machines, and the cyanide and everything."

"Great," I said. "Nobody can argue as good as you."

"CNN is interviewing the Indian group and me next week," she said.

That cyanide stuff is poison. People shouldn't be putting it in the soil where it can get in drinking water. What in heaven's name is the matter with their brains? People had been trying to correct laws governing the mining rights situation since 1988, but things were going mighty slow in Washington. The Canadian corporation's plan was perfectly legal as it stood. However, I had been doing some serious thinking. Unless these buzzards were intending to mine by helicopter, the only viable way in was either through my property, Faith Christine's, or one neighbor's—Oldman Reilly's property next to Christine's. I decided that I'd pay a visit to Oldman and see if he knew what was going on.

I said good-bye, got into my five-year-old blue Ford pickup, and drove on over to Oldman Reilly's place.

I parked, walked up to his screen door, and knocked. Oldman came to the screen door, greeted me with his usual friendly "Hi," and invited me in. We sat in his living room. Oldman was a small wiry man with thinning gray hair.

I sat in the armchair nearest the hallway to the back of the house, and he sat on the couch. I explained the situation to Oldman. Sure enough, a man had offered him five thousand dollars a year for "access" to the mountain through his property. Never mentioned mining. Wanted to put in an access road in on the far left edge of Oldman's property.

"Said they wanted to put it there so as not to bother me much, when they went in and out. They gave me the impression," he said, "without really saying it, now that I think about it, that they just wanted to use it for horseback riding for their family."

To Oldman, five grand seemed like a lot, and he seemed, at age eighty-five, to be unaware of the extent of what his permission would allow. I told him about chewing up the mountain to get the gold.

"I guess I'm gettin' old," he said. "I used to know enough to pull off the trail once in a while to see if the bad guys were behind me. Now it seems like I turned into a fool. I fell for their sweet talk; I could be bought for a few thousand dollars. I should have learned that lesson many years ago," he said bitterly.

"In the back of my mind I thought that that gent was too dressed up—in a new fancy black suit—to be a horseback-rider kind of man. But you know, with all the rich folks now in Silicon Valley, I thought that maybe they wanted to come up here weekends to get away or something. I'm sorry, John. I sure got fooled."

"Oldman, have you signed anything yet?"

"No, I ain't," he said, "but I give my word."

That was a serious thing to Oldman, I knew.

"What good is giving your word to a lyin' buzzard," I said. "They meant to pull the wool over your eyes. You don't owe them anything," I said angrily.

His eyes took on a happy gleam, lighting up the old wrinkled face at the thought of saving himself from "people only good for buzzard meat," as he said later.

He had his lawyer contact them, mentioning misrepresentation and fraud. This put a crimp in their plans. Meanwhile, Faith Christine and the TV reporters were doing their own detective work. The "buzzards" owning the mining company were silent partners in the Wall Street stock brokerage selling the mining stock. That's illegal.

The government people got strangely quiet about cutting off public access to Gray Mist. Suddenly they were very vague as to exactly whose idea it was. Nobody would take responsibility. In interview after interview, each person said it was somebody else's idea.

They re-interviewed Faith Christine on the six o'clock news talking about that fact. The Gray Mist deal fell through. The Wall Street participants headed for the hills, so to speak, with the law hot on their heels. I wasn't one bit sorry for them. "Pick up a rock and when the sunlight hits, the bugs scurry," I said to Faith Christine after they announced that the deal was officially dead.

"It was your idea about access to the mountain that saved us," she said as she poured me a cup of coffee in her kitchen where we were having chicken, mashed potatoes with gravy, and some of my broccoli.

"It was you who got the TV reporters hopped up enough to check on the behind-the-scenes finances," I said.

We had won. Faith Christine's prospectors had a reprieve, at least until varmints reappeared. But inside the fort the watch would be maintained. Faith Christine kept the hairdo; the business suits were going to be tucked away, she said. She looks good in the jeans and T-shirts, anyway. The cowboy boots are back—too hard to get mule muck off pumps.

We were sitting on her porch the next evening, enjoying the peace and quiet. Once in a while the brownish-gray mules in her corral next to the barn facing us brayed, but we didn't mind that. It was a spectacular evening, one in which you are especially glad to be alive.

"Like I told my kids," Faith Christine said, "in the end, it all boils down to one thing: either you're a survivor in life, or you're not. That's your two ultimate choices."

She looked at me, chuckling. "I've survived working with mules, almost being pushed off a mountain, and eating your darn vegetables."

I laughed. Then I said, "Faith Christine, we work well together."

"You're a good man," Faith Christine said. "I might be able to take a serious liking to you."

Always a gentleman, I said, "In the near future?"

She laughed.

"Right now," she said.

Chapter Three

It seems to me that after you first tell a woman you have strong feelings for her, you can expect to have a fight with her anywhere from right after to within the next eight days. I haven't had relationships with that many different women, but it seems to me that it holds true. Men are generally in a good mood after they've told someone that they like them a lot, and believe things will go along fine and good for a while, but women need to re-establish the "pecking order" or something. So they always, it seems to me, pick a fight.

Anyway, Faith Christine and I had our first big fight—not a long one, but certainly a loud and significant one—about one day after I realized we might be becoming more than friends. We had the fight at four o'clock Sunday afternoon, at her house, in her living room.

I had thought that we had been getting along just fine. But it seems she felt that I was not—well, I don't know what she called it, maybe I've purposely blocked it out—but she ended off by saying in a raised voice that I was too reserved and perhaps not moving ahead quickly enough in the romance department. Nothing could have been further from the truth, but I was raised to be reserved and a gentleman—and Dora had never complained. Faith Christine finished off by accusing me of being too "reticent."

I denied this, but shortly after hearing that, I left Faith Christine's house to go home and think about it.

I had a pretty good idea what reticent meant, but when I got home, I went to my pine bookcase in the living room, got the *Webster's Dictionary* out, sat down in my old green armchair near the window facing Gray Mist, and looked it up to find out specifically. " 'Reticent,' " I read aloud. " 'Keeping one's own counsel; habitually silent, refraining from talking, taciturn, reserved.' " I looked up taciturn. It said it meant "reticent," and "habitually silent, not apt to talk."

That didn't mean moving too slowly in a relationship, I thought angrily. Just like a woman to mix these things up. Not talking didn't equate with taking things slowly at first. Maybe just the opposite.

It had been a long time since my wife died, and I had a lot of—well, feelings—saved up. I was having a hard time knowing how to treat Faith Christine. I didn't want to scare her off. But also, I had been raised to be a gentleman. A smart woman would prefer a gentleman in the long run to a rough-and-tumble rascal, I still felt, grumbling angrily to myself, sitting there, staring out the window for a long time. And maybe feeling a little sorry for myself, to tell the honest truth.

Hmm. I thought some more. I calmed down. A little. Faith Christine wanted me to be more forthcoming about my feelings for her. Dora had always taken the lead; she was the romantic one. Okay, next time—okay, maybe right now—I'd go over there and grab Faith Christine (gently, of course) and give her a big wild kiss. And see if that was what she meant. And I'd talk, dangit, while I was doing it. If it killed me.

The phone rang, jarring my thoughts.

"John, is that you?" a voice asked.

"Yes," I said, wondering who it was, but vaguely recognizing the deep voice.

"This is Jerry Vivens," the voice said, and immediately I placed him. Police. What was he doing calling me?

"I'm over at Oldman's place. He's been knifed."

Oh, God, I thought. "Is he all right?" I said.

"No. He's been stabbed seventeen or eighteen times."

"Oh, my," I said. Immediately, I felt guilty. I didn't know why, but I felt it was at least partly my fault for dragging him into the mess about Gray Mist. Somebody had gotten even. We'd cost someone millions of dollars; obviously they had retaliated.

"Is somebody over at Faith Christine's?" I said, my first thoughts that maybe she might be next.

"On the way," Jerry said, comforting me somewhat. "In fact, should be there by now."

"Do you think it's because of the big fight we've all been in lately, Jerry?" I asked. "About the mountain, I mean—about the big mining deal that fell through because of what we did? I mean the investigation and Faith Christine's being on TV and talking against it."

"I have no idea. Could be, though. Faith Christine was

on the news a lot. I even saw her on CNN a couple of times. Some of the men she went up against are rich and powerful and used to getting their own way. They might not take too kindly to being exposed."

The line was silent for a moment.

"I was wondering if you could come over and take a look," Jerry said. "You knew Oldman as well as anybody. Somebody here in the office said that you go over once a week to check on him, see if he's all right. Is that true?"

"Yes."

"Could you come over and take a look around—see if anything is missing or disturbed? None of the police around here have ever been in his house before."

"Certainly," I said. "Be there in a couple of minutes."

I called Faith Christine. She said that a policeman was already there and she was safe. "I tried to call you but the line was busy," she said.

"I'm on my way over to Oldman's," I told her.

I got in my Ford, turned left at the end of my driveway, and drove down the little-used two-lane road past Faith Christine's driveway and on down the road toward Oldman's house. Faith Christine has a fence to keep her mules on her property, but the fencing along the road ends where Oldman's property begins. I arrived at Oldman's property line shortly after that, drove a little farther, and turned into Oldman's long dirt driveway. I had trouble finding a place to park. Police cars and vans were parked all over the place, almost all the way out to the road. Yellow police tape all around the place. Jerry came out and handed me covers for my shoes even before I got out of my truck.

Jerry's a medium-sized, stocky man, well-muscled.

I was pretty certain that he'd never handled a murder

case before. The crime around here is usually limited to an occasional teenage prank or minor burglary or someone's animals escaping onto someone else's property when a fence is down.

A month ago a mountain lion attacked a young woman— a jogger—who was jogging alone in some foothills about twenty miles from here, but she got away by yelling and hitting the animal in the eyes. Animal experts said that her jogging "triggered a hunting reflex" in the lion. Not exactly a criminal case.

"I don't want to screw up this investigation," Jerry said, referring to the plastic shoe covers. "Sorry. You'll need to put them on when we reach the door of the house."

"No problem," I said. "I'll carry the shoe covers with me till we get to the door."

He dug again in his pocket. "You won't be touching anything, but here are some gloves to put on. We're finished with the crime scene photos."

He handed the latex gloves to me as I sat in the Ford with the driver's side door open, and I put them on, feeling like a doctor about to operate. I grabbed the shoe covers, got out, and shut the truck door. I was feeling sorry for Oldman Reilly, if I was considered his best friend.

I had known him for twenty years in a neighborly way, but I had never, in that period of time, really talked to him intimately about his personal life or problems.

We talked the usual small talk: "How're you feeling this week? How's everybody?" I'd ask.

Oldman would say, "Good." We talked about the weather, our gardens, tools, how his truck was running. Stuff like that. Perhaps the closest I had gotten to him was recently, in the squabble over Gray Mist. It was a sad commentary, in a way, about how distant we are sometimes, from even our most immediate neighbors. And there was a thirty-year age difference. I had a lot more in common with Faith Christine.

And here in Northern California, our "immediate" neighbors were at a distance, mostly miles apart. Most of us wanted it that way or we'd be living somewhere else.

I was further surprised when Jerry said that from a quick preliminary search of Oldman's papers, I was listed as the executor of his will. "Doesn't Oldman have a son?" I asked, surprised, shocked, and I must admit, not too pleased to hear this news. I would have liked it if I was at least asked first.

"Something funny going on there, I think," Jerry said, as we walked toward the house. I knew Oldman had a lawyer. Why wasn't he the executor?

Inside and outside, policemen—I should say police persons, there were a few women in uniform—in one capacity or another were milling around. More people than I had ever seen in Oldman's house in all the years I'd known him. I could see them through the windows.

"Kept to himself a lot, Oldman did," Jerry said.

I nodded. "He was a private man. A good man, though," I added, "as far as I know. Never gave anybody any trouble, and did the right thing, as far as I am concerned, about old Gray Mist."

"Might have got him killed, doing the right thing," Jerry said.

I saw a policewoman with a video camera come out the door of the house. Evidence videos. I felt terrible.

The point of the roof of Oldman's gray house faced us as we walked toward his house; the entrance door was in the center, and one window was on either side. Late-day shadows made the faded house look sad and rather depressing.

The window on the left side of the door was in the kitchen; the window on the right side was in the living room. No shutters. No decorations of any kind. No woman's touches. The house of a man who had lived alone many years. Reddish dirt, rocky front yard, and just a dirt road leading to his isolated driveway and house.

In fact, the main road came to an end about a mile and a half past Oldman's driveway. One more house was down there, on the opposite side of the road from mine, Faith Christine's, and Oldman's. The last house belonged to a widow named Esther Cooper. She kept chickens and sold eggs to local families.

Oldman's battered dark-brown Toyota truck was parked next to the house where the driveway ended.

There was a small unlocked shed behind the house of weathered wood. Inside were a few tools and things. The last time I was in it was three weeks ago. Oldman and I had been talking about tools and we walked into his shed for him to show me a saw he was very proud of. It was a saw that had belonged to his father. His father had been a carpenter.

Now that I thought about it, that was the only time I had ever seen Oldman express any strong emotion, other than that day we were talking about Gray Mist and the miners' ploy to trick him into allowing them access.

Oldman's house looked like it was built in the twenties, no—maybe thirties. Needed work, inside and out.

When Jerry and I reached the front doorstep I stopped to put the "booties" on that I was carrying. They covered my size eleven black leather handtooled cowboy boots only as far up as the heels, but that was evidently enough.

Jerry nodded approval and opened the screen door. He had put his own booties on at the same time I did.

The dirt-smudged inside white wooden door was already open. The screen door in front of it had a small three-corner tear in it that had been there for years.

Jerry reached around and opened the screen door for me. I entered and Jerry followed me inside into the small living room. A much-used gray couch stood in the middle of the wall on the right. Two mission-style oak end tables, with tarnished, mismatched brass lamps—one tall, one short— were on either side of the couch. Yellowed fly-specked shades on the lamps; one shade on crooked. A few old magazines and newspapers were tossed on a dilapidated brown Formica coffee table with chrome legs in front of the couch. Probably cost twenty-nine dollars thirty years ago.

A textured brown, out-of-style, wide-armed armchair looking like it had—barely—survived from the fifties, sat with its back near the hallway to the bedrooms, bathroom, and the back of the house. It was the chair I usually sat in when I came to visit. A black metal floor lamp with another yellowed shade stood near it.

A couple of cheap pictures were on the wall. No rug— probably because of the dirt and dust constantly tracked in from outside. Oldman was practical, if nothing else. You could take the broom and sweep the dust and dirt back outside through the front door.

A twenty-year-old Sharp television sitting on a chrome stand was in the front right corner of the room, more facing the armchair than the couch. You could have written your name in the dust on the screen. Fine dust blew in through the mesh of the windowscreens. The windows were open.

Everything looked normal so far, in this part of the house.

I knew there were only five rooms in the small house, not counting the bathroom. The doorway to the small kitchen was to the left, off the living room, through a wide arch.

"Do you know of anybody specifically who was so angry about—you know, the whole business—that they might have wanted him killed?" Jerry said, his heavy blond eyebrows knit together in concern as we walked slowly through the living room.

We walked straight back, up the short hall past ugly gray, at least forty-year-old wallpaper on both sides of us. Large dark gray feather-like plumes on a light gray background.

The first door I saw on the left past the kitchen door was the door to the small bathroom. I'd been in his bathroom before. The door was open and somebody was in there now, investigating.

I'd never been up the hall past the bathroom in all the years I'd known Oldman, although I knew that there were two small bedrooms on the left side of the hall, and a larger one on the other. I said so. Then I answered his question.

"Not around here," I said. It was the truth. People around here had supported our fight, almost to a man.

Jerry nodded agreement, then he said, "Of course, you know, in this kind of crime, up close and personal, so to speak, nine out of ten times it is a family member—or someone who knew the victim," he said.

Then he looked directly at me, and I knew he was watching for my reaction. Faith Christine had mentioned once that he would have been movie-star handsome if it weren't for the fact that his nose is a little too pointy on the very end.

"Who stands to profit from his death?" Jerry said. "You got any idea?"

I shook my head.

"Oldman didn't seem like the kind of man anyone would get that mad at," I said. "He was kind of low-key. Who is his beneficiary?" I asked, after thinking a second. I added, "I don't think Oldman had any money. And I doubt if this—pardon my saying it—run-down house is worth killing him for, either," I added.

"It must be his son, I would guess," Jerry said, in regard to my beneficiary question. He relaxed a little—breathed out—and I could feel that I had passed some test.

"Alice, at the station, is trying to get ahold of Oldman's lawyer. He's out of town today. You didn't know that you were executor?"

"Jerry, I didn't have a clue." I hoped he'd read the expression on my face and realize that I wasn't too happy about finding out that I was the executor. I had the distinctly uncomfortable feeling that I had only recently become the executor. Probably *after* the business about the mountain and the mining company. It sounded like something the old man would do. He'd been real concerned that the miners never get their hands on his property after the way they'd tried to do it by lying about the reason for the right-of-way onto the mountain. "Lying sons of B's," he'd called them, the last time we'd spoken of it.

We continued up the short hall, into the back bedroom on the right at the far end of the hall.

The doorway to the back bedroom looked small and narrow when Jerry's broad shoulders walked through it. Black stuff that I assumed must be for finding fingerprints was on the doorway and the door and we were both careful not to brush up against anything.

This bedroom was larger than I expected. The two across the hall must be very small, owing to the bathroom using up some of that space, I guessed.

"Who could be that angry with him—enough to do this?" he said. "The man was eighty-five, for God's sake!"

I walked cautiously into the bedroom where Oldman lay sprawled across his bedspread. Most of the wounds looked to be in the chest, but some were on his hands. In real life, I had never seen much blood, only on TV programs and movies. It was a little different color than I expected. Darker.

Chapter Four

I'd seen my share of dead people before, but they were all neat and clean and straight, laid out in hospital beds or in caskets—including my wife, my parents, aunts and uncles, and even Faith Christine's husband.

None of them like this—sprawled, one leg hanging off the dingy old white bedspread. At least the bedspread used to be white.

Although he'd died in the bedroom, Oldman was fully dressed. He must have run back here to get away from his attacker. Maybe thought that he could get to the bedroom and lock the door. Be safe.

But it didn't work out that way. Obviously.

I didn't want to have Jerry and the other people in the room see me "freak out," as my kids would say. I tried to act cool.

"Who found him?" I asked. I looked at the dresser, the

26

wallpaper (ugly faded green ferns), and everywhere else but back at Oldman.

The bed, night tables, and two dressers were mission style, same as the living room. Yellowed fly-specked lamp-shades. A dented black metal wastebasket near the bed, filled with used tissues. Half-empty box of tissues on one of the night tables near the bed.

"Esther Cooper. She delivers—delivered—him a dozen eggs every two weeks. When she got here, the door was open, and she walked in and found—this. She was pretty upset. I had to send her home."

I could picture Esther, a little old lady with white hair, delivering her eggs, coming in, and finding this.

She was in her late seventies, I guessed. Very spry for her age. She left your eggs on your front doorstep if you weren't home. You paid her once a month. Could mail her a check if you didn't want to drive down to her house to pay her. Oldman usually left her cash in an envelope on the first Tuesday of each month, I knew. He'd leave it in the space between the screen door and the inside door. If it was raining, he'd leave it in a plastic bag.

"It must have been terrible for her. She's a nice old lady," I said.

I felt helpless. I knew next to nothing about Oldman's personal life and troubles—if he had any—other than our recent ones about the mining rights.

I looked around the bedroom again. There wasn't much sign of a struggle, not that I expected much of one. Oldman probably weighed a hundred and ten pounds.

Just the cuts on his hands. The cuts told me he had not given up living without a fight, at eighty-five. Courage.

If it was a hit—someone out of New York City, or

Washington, or the Canadian mining guys—I would have expected Oldman to have been shot. Not this bloody mess.

"The person doing this must have gotten bloody," I said. Jerry nodded.

"When, exactly, did it happen?" I said, feeling a bad headache starting across my forehead.

"Don't know yet. I need someone with a little more experience to say," Jerry said honestly. "My best guess is last evening." I had to give him credit for being honest, and not trying to show off and be a big shot. He knew he needed help on this one from people with more experience.

"I need to locate his son right away," Jerry said. "Any clues as to where he might be?"

I shook my head. "I need an aspirin," I said.

"Can't run the water yet," Jerry said, trying to smile. "You'll have to suffer."

I nodded. Of course. They would be searching the drains for blood. Taking everything apart.

Together we walked back outside and stood outside the house about five feet from the front doorsteps. It was a relief. I realized that I had been partly holding my breath inside.

"You think Faith Christine's in danger?" I said.

Jerry took out a small black cell phone from a chest pocket. He flipped it open, shaking his head in an "I don't know" kind of way.

"Here. It's my own. Call. Check on her, if it'll make you feel better." He flipped it open, pulled up the antenna, pressed a button, and handed the phone to me.

"Thanks," I said.

"Faith Christine," I said after pressing the buttons for her number with the plastic gloves still on my hands, holding the small strange object close to my head and feeling fool-ishly modern.

Where's the comforting bottom mouthpiece you speak into, like on a regular phone? This small black rectangle came only halfway down my face. How could she hear me? She sounded small and far away, but maybe I'm too old-fashioned and picky about modern things.

"Are you all right? Is the policeman still there?"

"Yes and yes," she said. "You sound funny. Are you all right?"

I was relieved that she didn't sound mad anymore. About the "reticent" thing. In fact, she sounded relieved to hear my voice. "Sorry about the fight," she said. "You sound funny."

"I'm on a cell phone, here at Oldman's. It's Jerry's phone," I said. "I'll talk to you later," I said awkwardly, and then I hung up. Or, well, I would have. I handed the phone back to Jerry and he did what was necessary to shut the thing off.

There I was, being taciturn again, but Jerry was standing there listening. "She's fine," I said to Jerry, feeling guilty because I was suspecting him of lending me the phone on purpose so he could listen.

Did he suspect me? He hadn't acted so far as if he did; but in his shoes, I might. I studied Jerry more carefully.

I knew that I was innocent.

He closed the phone up into a remarkably small rectangle and put it away, back into that same pocket.

I knew that I felt sorry—and guilty—about the man in-side that faded house that was badly in need of a painting. Maybe I ought to have offered to paint it as a neighborly thing. Too late now. "I want to help," I said. "But I don't know what to do, or how," I finished lamely.

I almost felt that he wanted to say, "Me, too."

Instead he drew himself up to his highest height, and tried to look professional. He reassured himself by fingering his gun. I had known Jerry for a long time.

He had always had that faint "keep your distance" attitude that all policemen have to develop for their own safety. They deal with liars too much.

I wondered if he thought *I* was lying.

"We'll know more as soon as we locate his lawyer and his son," Jerry said. "Hang around, if you can, John—as soon as the guys are finished inside I want you to help me take a closer look around. Like I said on the phone, see if anything appears missing."

On my way in, I'd looked quickly, but it looked as if things were pretty normal. All except in the back bedroom. I said so.

"All the same, I'd appreciate it if you'd wait in your truck over there," Jerry said.

I did. I got in, took off the plastic gloves and booties, laid them on the passenger side seat, and closed the door.

I would have cleaned out my ashtrays or my glove compartment to help pass the time, but I didn't want to inadvertently screw up or disturb evidence in the yard.

Time passed slowly. I didn't want to leave, anyway, leaving Oldman alone in there with only police—mostly strangers—in there. It was the least I could do to sit there; in a way I was keeping him company by sitting there in his yard.

It seemed like there were about twenty million people inside. Were they all necessary? Plumbing tools were being brought inside. How many were just curious and wanted to be there at the scene of a murder?

It was a long time before men carried out Oldman's body—close to nine o'clock. My stomach was growling before Jerry came and got me.

He gave me new shoe covers and gloves when we got to the door. I walked back inside, as I had before, into the living room.

I tried to picture how everything was the last time I was in Oldman's house before today. Trouble is, I never pay too much attention to decorations and things like that.

No darker spots on the faded wallpaper jumped out at me—I could see nothing missing there, and if any small household decorations were missing, I couldn't tell, although I looked to see if there were any clean spots in the sandy-looking light layer of dust on the tabletops. The police had dusted everywhere for fingerprints during their long stay.

I walked into the kitchen.

"Heard you're seeing a lot of Faith Christine these days," Jerry said, following me into the kitchen. "That woman is a saint," he said feelingly. "When my mother was sick, she brought over dinner I don't know how many times," he said.

I wondered what he would say if I told him "the saint" was complaining that I wasn't "romantic" enough.

The kitchen was about as dirty as mine. I'm not too good about cleaning corners, although I do try to wipe things off from time to time. Toaster full of crumbs.

Oldman's floor was normally a little sandy—dirt tracked in from outside, same as at my place—but now it had been all vacuumed up by the police.

Two sets of dirty cups and saucers on the table. I looked. One that had been sitting there for a long time, and one more recent? Or two about the same age?

To tell the truth, I couldn't tell. The milk hadn't formed a ring yet, like some dirty cups of mine did when I left them too long before washing them. Well, I wasn't supposed to be a detective here, just an observer.

I tried to imprint everything in my mind. Maybe later something would come to me. Sometimes that was the way my mind worked, these days. Old age. Started a year ago when I turned fifty.

"I can't see anything different or missing, right off," I said to Jerry. He was watching me like a hawk. "Not here in the kitchen."

"Let's walk through again," he suggested. We did.

We started in the tiny back left bedroom, where Oldman had a rather large oak desk crammed in. Took up a lot of space. The bed had been removed to fit it in. Jerry didn't want me to look through that.

In fact, I wasn't to touch anything. The bedroom was small like I'd thought. I looked around, but I'd already told Jerry I'd never been in there before and wouldn't know if anything was missing. It looked like an old man's spare room that he used to pay his bills and do his income tax.

"Maybe something that you've seen Oldman with, that is gone, might pop into your head," he said.

We went back across the hallway into the other now-empty, silent larger bedroom—bedspread, sheets, blankets, and a lot of stuff were gone. Oldman was gone. Pieces of the mattress cut out. A bedroom that Oldman would never sleep in again. He was on his way to being autopsied.

We went back across the hall into the other small middle

bedroom. That still had a twin-size bed in it. The walls were a dull gray, and the blanket on the bed had gray-and-white stripes in a kind of Indian-like design.

We went into the bathroom, then the living room, and finally ended up back in the kitchen again. There was nothing that jumped out at me as missing.

"No liquor in the house," Jerry said, looking around the small kitchen. "Someone already checked."

Old-fashioned gray Formica table, the cups now gone. The last police officer, who just left, must have just removed them. Even though the table was small, it took up most of the room. Pine cabinets, gray Formica countertop. Plain white curtains on the window.

"I never saw Oldman with a drink in his hand, come to think of it," I said.

"What a life," Jerry said expressionlessly, looking around the fifties-style kitchen. Someone had done a little remodeling in the fifties.

"Sorry, Jerry," I said, frowning. "Maybe later I'll remember something."

A stomach growled loudly.

"Was that yours or mine?" I asked.

"Mine, I'm afraid," Jerry said. "I felt it."

"Were there any prints on the teacups?"

He shook his head, no.

We walked to the front door. He turned off all the lights.

Before we left, he summoned in a very young cop who had been outside, waiting. The young cop was evidently going to spend the night.

Jerry indicated for me to stand there, outside on the steps, and he went and got a flashlight out of his police cruiser, and took me out to look in the shed.

There was fresh evidence that a mouse or mice had taken up living in there. Other than that, everything looked the same in there. I shook my head.

Jerry obviously felt that he couldn't be too careful. He closed the door of the shed, and we walked toward my truck, stepping over the yellow police tape.

I thought it was very strange to worry about leaving this property empty overnight—way the heck out here in the boondocks where only four of us lived: Oldman, Faith Christine, Esther, and me. Nobody much ever came out near here at night.

Unless Jerry knew something I didn't.

Maybe he thought that the murderer would come back.

On the way back to my car, I noticed a fresh-looking Budweiser beer bottle lying off to the side of the driveway, about twenty feet from my car. It was almost hidden in the grass.

I pointed it out to Jerry, and he picked it up using a pencil down the neck and put it in a plastic bag as evidence. I could see that he was annoyed that his men had missed it. I figured someone was going to get chewed out when he got back to the police station, by the look on his face.

"Thanks," he said.

Chapter Five

I was back in my truck and halfway home—or actually on my way to Faith Christine's—before I realized that Jerry hadn't mentioned Faith Christine's prospectors. Could one of them have circled down and killed Oldman? Her prospectors certainly didn't seem the type; still, you never knew. I was certain Jerry would check on any prospectors out on Gray Mist.

Who killed Oldman?

I was pretty sure it wasn't a sex crime, or a crime of passion. Not with Oldman. You never knew, of course. Stranger things have happened.

Money? Greed?

Drugs were out as a possibility.

More likely something to do with the mining business.

Was someone else more able to see an advantage to be

gained by his death? Something so complex that my brain didn't see as a possibility?

Had he abused his family?

I knew so little about his family, I was not in a position to even take a guess.

Yet, my gut feeling was that Oldman Reilly was a simple, rather than a complex man. Not a complicated, devious man.

Yet, he didn't drink—not even one drop. Sometimes that indicated a man who had a problem with it earlier in life. And that can cause serious troubles with relationships that can spill over into later years.

Maybe I was too cynical. That was something I lived with from having been a New York lawyer in my past life.

I pulled into Faith Christine's very familiar yard. A Rushing River Junction police cruiser was parked too near her porch.

I would have parked further back than that. The cruiser would give excellent cover to anyone sneaking up on the house. A figure profiled himself in the light of the door.

"Dang," I said to myself. A kid cop.

"That's a nice target you make," I said as fakely pleasantly as I could through gritted teeth as I reached the porch, crossed it, and almost rudely pushed past him to see Faith Christine.

She gave me a warning look with her raised eyebrows: be polite. The hell with that, I said to myself.

"If someone is out there, that cruiser will give him cover sneaking up on the house," I said fiercely to the kid.

"John, this is Betty Denton's boy," she said, pursing her lips at me in additional warning. "He's new on the force," she said.

I recognized him from town, now that I looked at him more closely. Knew his mother.

"You move that cruiser?" I said firmly, my voice saying do it and do it now, even though I'd pretended to politely phrase it as a question.

He nodded and went outside.

"Shut off the inside roof light if it's on automatic," I said.

"It's not," he said, sounding frankly relieved that some-one was taking over.

"He's only a kid," Faith Christine said fiercely, in a way that meant "leave him alone."

"He's only a kid," I repeated. "That's just great. Jerry sends a kid to take care of you."

"That's all he had available, probably. Everyone else was over at Oldman's."

"That's true. Everyone was there except the President of the United States and Mickey Mouse."

"What's the matter with you?"

"I'm tired, hungry, and ticked off. Oldman is dead. You might be next. I might be next after you. We have a baby policeman out there. Why should anything be the matter with me? Oh, and I'm not romantic enough. Is that enough for one day?"

"Boy, you're grouchy. I think you're hungry. Come on in the kitchen and I'll make you a sandwich."

She thought for a minute and then squinted her eyes fiercely at me and said, "And I can take care of myself, thank you very much."

"Can you take care of yourself and that kid, too?" I said. She didn't answer. We walked into the kitchen. Ken, the policeboy, walked back in a moment later.

"Ken, go get a blanket off one of the beds, and hang it in front of the picture window, will you?"

He looked sorry that he hadn't thought of that and disappeared.

I noticed two cups—mugs—already sitting on the table. It reminded me of the two cups and saucers I saw at Oldman's, and a pain pierced my heart.

Ken came back with a pale-blue blanket, which we hung across the window. We asked Faith Christine's permission and used two small nails. She had never hung a curtain over the kitchen window that looked toward the mountain, so there weren't any curtain rod holders up.

This took a couple of minutes. Kid had never used a hammer before, obviously. Kind of comical. I held the blanket while the kid insisted on wielding the hammer. Only hit his finger once. Stopped to suck his finger three times. Didn't do any real damage to his finger, luckily.

"There were two cups and saucers out at Oldman's," I said to the two of them, as we finished and the kid and I sat down at the table.

Faith Christine busied herself working at the counter. "Have they gotten hold of Oldman's kids?" she asked.

"Kids?" I said. "I thought Oldman only had a son. One son."

She looked over at me as if I were crazy as she got me a mug, filled it with coffee, and set it down in front of me. Then she brought over a huge stuffed sandwich from her counter. Whole-grain bread. I stuffed a big bite into my mouth. Roast beef. I had to chew a bit before I could answer. Lettuce, tomato, cheddar cheese, mustard. Ah. "This is good," I said, chewing.

"What?" Faith Christine said.

"This is good," I said, able to talk more clearly by chewing and then drinking a big swig of her great coffee.

She sat next to me and sipped her own coffee.

Suddenly, I felt tired, but more relaxed. "Ken, how's your mother?" I asked.

"Fine," he said, apparently not mad at me for yelling before. Sometimes young people expect people my age to be grouchy and yell, and take it well; that surprises me, as I could never get away like this with being grouchy when I was young. One of the "perks" of being fifty.

Ken was one of the kids I taught when I was in charge of the high school rodeo every year. His mother helped me. She's a nice woman.

"You shouldn't have given up doing the rodeo," Ken said. "The kids liked you. They hate the guy who does it now, and he's quitting. Membership is down since you stopped doing it," Ken said unexpectedly. "Only ten kids now."

Faith Christine raised her eyebrows at me in an "I told you so" way.

I drank again. There were twenty to twenty-five kids when I did it.

"Ken, how long have you been on the police force?" I asked.

"About six weeks," he said.

Great, I said to myself.

"Ken, until we know who it was who killed Mr. Reilly, we have to be careful. They may go after Mrs. Butler next."

He nodded intently, and I realized that he had learned something. He would be careful from now on. But dang it, he looked so young.

"Faith, you said 'kids?' I thought there was only one son—Charles."

Now they both raised their eyebrows at me.

"Mr. and Mrs. Oldman had two children," Ken said. "There was an older daughter nobody saw much. Kept to herself. There was something wrong with her, I think."

Faith Christine bobbed her head in agreement. She knew about everybody. "Charles is in a drug rehab in Los Angeles somewhere. I'm not sure where Beth is," she added. I could tell she was not telling everything.

"What?" I asked, looking at her. She looked tired, but her cheeks were red.

"I don't know if I should tell . . ."

"What, for Pete's sake? Oldman is dead," I said. "What's the big secret?"

She looked at Ken. He was silent, waiting.

"Beth has been ill, off and on. Psychological troubles. I don't know if something happened to her or what. She's been under psychiatric care off and on. Since she was quite young. That's why you probably don't remember her. She spent most of her life in institutions. Since she was about eight, I think."

"Is she out now?" Ken asked.

"I don't know. The last few years I've lost track of her whereabouts."

I felt sorry for Oldman. He wasn't wealthy, and he had his hands full with his children. One with psychiatric problems, the other in drug rehab. I felt a strong rush of relief and love that my own children were fine.

Then I glanced over at Faith Christine and was glad that her children were fine, also.

I looked at Ken. He was a fine boy, too. I was proud of

him, too. Suddenly, we were a group, the three of us. We all looked at one another.

"Ken's here for the night," Faith Christine said. "And I expect you are, too, if you want. Ken's got the side bedroom on the left. You can have the one on the right, next to mine," she said, grinning at me. "I already made it up."

"You knew that I'd come," I said.

"One way or another," she said, chuckling, "I knew you'd be back." She was referring to the fight.

"Are we going to take watches?" Ken asked, looking at me.

"Probably should," I said. "It couldn't hurt."

"I'll go first," Ken said. "I'll wake you when I get tired . . . and I'll stay away from lighted doors and windows," he said, looking at me intently.

He went to sit in the living room, taking his mug of coffee. I watched him as he left, nearly six foot tall, with closely cropped policeman-like dark brown hair. His face was still the friendly, open face of a kid.

Too bad what being a policeman would do to that face over the years. And his attitude about the innate goodness of people. In fact, his most likeable feature was his innocence, although it had irritated me earlier.

I stood in the doorway between the kitchen and the living room as he carefully closed all the drapes on the other windows.

He turned toward me and said, "I'm smart and I'll learn."

I looked directly at him. "I know that." Boy, did I know that. I'd just come from a bloody crime scene. I hoped he'd never have to look at anything like that. Nobody should. I'd never forget it.

Ken had been sent here, instead. If he'd seen what I'd

seen today, already that face would be just a little different. Maybe Jerry was sparing him a while longer, but I doubted it. It wasn't Jerry's style. He was an in-your-face, up-front realist. Had to be.

I returned to the kitchen.

Faith Christine was cleaning up.

"You want some canned peaches?"

"No."

"More coffee?"

"Yes." I sat. "Sit," I said. She got the coffee and sat next to me again. She put her hand on my shoulder.

"Sorry I was so grouchy before," she said quietly. "This constitutes a big change in my life, in the status quo, so to speak." I knew she was referring to the change in our relationship. "It's a little scary," she added. "I've been alone for a few years now."

"You're different than Dora," I said. "You'll take some getting used to," I joked.

"So will you," she said, smiling.

"I could tell right off that you like Ken," she said, withdrawing her hand, sitting up straight and changing the subject. "Even if you were grouching at him when you arrived."

"He seems like a nice kid," I agreed.

"He is. What did you see at Oldman's?"

"Nothing too exciting . . . I don't mean that—I mean I didn't see anything obvious missing. I felt bad. Oldman obviously fought the guy off; his hands were stabbed, it looked like. Nothing seemed to be stolen—not that Oldman had anything much to steal," I said. "No stereo, CD player, cell phone, computer or anything. I don't think he had much—or any money."

"People like Oldman sometimes have large stashes of cash."

"That's true. But I think he needed every penny to live on. He drove a beat-up old vehicle."

"You never know. But he could have sold his antique oak furniture. That's worth something these days."

"You might be right. I never liked antiques that much."

"In Los Angeles, or San Francisco, that oak furniture would bring big bucks."

"Did you know Oldman had made me executor of his will?"

Surprisingly, she nodded.

"You knew?" I said, completely shocked for the second or third time that day.

"How come you never told me?" I said, annoyed.

"He asked me not to."

I knew that Faith Christine never betrayed a confidence. Still, I was irked. I expected loyalty. I said so.

"You old poop!" she said fondly, not the least bit annoyed at my annoyance. "Besides, I think Oldman was smart to choose you. Didn't I choose you, too?" she added, smiling wickedly.

"What about his own lawyer, or his son, or his daughter?"

"No, no, and definitely no."

"No relatives or other friends?"

"No. He's a grouchy cuss—or was. Like us. He probably felt that we understood him better than anybody, because we also chose this same isolated lifestyle."

She looked at me. "You look awful. You look all tired, and you need a shave." She gave me a peck on my unshaven cheek.

Even at my age I have terrible five-o'clock shadow. Black hair, black beard. I haven't grown a beard in many years, so I'm not sure if it would come in gray now. But it still looks pretty dark on my chin and jaws if I'm the least bit lazy about shaving.

Faith Christine has said before, more than once, that she likes my green eyes. She says they are "friendly eyes," and crinkle at the corners when I smile. I think it's just plain old wrinkles, to tell the truth.

I finished my coffee, then we went to our separate rooms.

Just before I fell asleep I realized that in all of Oldman's whole house, I hadn't seen one photograph or picture of his wife, his son, or his daughter. Or him. Anywhere.

Unless they were in that big oak desk in the small back bedroom. Later, as executor, I'd have to go through all that stuff in the desk.

Had there been any photographs there before, on previous visits to his house? I racked my brain, trying to remember. There were so many unanswered questions. I didn't remember seeing any, but I'm not one to spend a lot of time looking at decorations in people's houses. I fell asleep until I heard the door opening to the bedroom where I was sleeping, and a few seconds later Ken tapped me gently on the shoulder to wake me up.

"Mr. Ranger," he said, "it's your turn on watch."

I took the one-to-five watch. It was quiet. Nothing happened. I let Ken sleep until six.

Chapter Six

Iwoke Ken up, and then went to bed. At eight-thirty I got up and dressed. I looked terrible. Again.

There was breakfast food set out, and there was a full pot of coffee in the white plastic drip pot sitting on the kitchen counter. I poured myself a cup, added milk and sugar, and sipped it. I rolled the blue blanket into a bumpy lump above the window so that I could look out at the mountain for a minute. Oldman would never be looking at this mountain again. Who would be moving into his house? One of his kids? Would they be our neighbors now, sharing the view with us instead of him? Or would they sell it?

I knew Oldman had recently put a clause in his will that I had first right of refusal of anyone purchasing his property as a protection against miners buying it in a roundabout way if he got incapacitated or senile. Maybe the killers— the mining corporation—thought that if Oldman was killed, the house would come on the market and they could purchase it and gain access to the mountain.

If his children wanted to keep it and/or live there, I wouldn't have to worry about that. If they moved out here, what would they do for a living?

Did Oldman have insurance? I didn't know squat about his business. I guessed the lawyer would be getting in touch with me today. For that, I'd need to go home. But I didn't want to leave Faith Christine alone.

If Jerry were here, or an older cop . . .

Faith Christine had other ideas. She came into the kitchen with her purse. "Let's go," she said, snapping the switch on the coffeepot to the OFF position. The red light went out.

"I already pulled your bed together," she said, all businesslike. "And Ken is outside."

I finished my coffee; I didn't feel like eating yet. "Come on," she said. "We're going to your house."

I got my stuff and followed her outside, making sure the door was locked as I closed it.

She walked over and hung a large CLOSED sign up on a hook she had near her barn, and as she walked back, she said, "Ken looked after the mules."

I could see that. They were eating and drinking in her corral near the barn. The barn door inside the corral was open so they could go in and out the door on the side of the barn as they wished.

In a way I was relieved. I needed a change of clothes, a shower, and a shave. I felt like a grunge.

Ken saw us coming out as he reached the cruiser, and waved at us as he opened the door and got in. Seconds later, he drove off.

"He's going to check in at the police station. He said he'll be back later," she told me.

"Phew," Faith Christine said a few minutes later as we entered my house. "Don't you believe in dusting?"

"Been busy," I grumbled. "I do keep the TV screen washed, and the toilet and bathtub clean," I said, annoyed that I have to explain myself to another human being. "And don't you start cleaning," I said, like an animal defending my territory.

She understood perfectly. "I won't touch anything, believe me."

"I got to shower," I said, ignoring that remark.

The warm water felt wonderful, and soothed my aching bones. I didn't want to ever get out, but finally I did. I rubbed down with one of the thick towels still left from when my wife was living. She'd always insisted on good, thick fluffy towels. Tended to whites, pinks, and pale blues as color choices for towels. Everything color-coordinated in the house when she was living. Dora had loved all kinds of tablecloths and linens. The hall closet near the formal dining room to the right of the kitchen at the back of the house was still chock full of them. I never opened that closet. Couldn't bear to. Now, I left both the kitchen and the dining room tables plain, with bare wood showing. No tablecloth. Both tables had gotten some marks and dings and cup rings on them since she'd died.

I shaved, and then I got dressed in clean clothes, and threw the dirty ones in the hamper.

Faith Christine was sitting on the couch when I came out. "I thought at our age life was going to be—supposed to be—boring," she said.

I was taciturn. Maybe reticent, even. I needed time to think about Oldman's murder.

We checked on all my livestock, and did what we needed to do in a comfortable silence. Or, at least, in reasonable enough comfort, considering all that had happened lately.

We saddled up my horses and checked fences to be sure that they were not down as we rode. When we got back, we took care of the horses and went back into the house.

We decided to go back to her house and walked out onto the porch. I was just about to reach around and lock the door, when the phone rang. She went back inside to answer it. Coming back, she stood in the doorway and said quietly, "Lawyer." I passed by her into the living room, and picked up the phone.

"George Finley, here." There was a pompous tone to his voice. Right away I didn't like him.

"John Ranger, here," I said, emphasizing the "here."

There was silence for a moment, then he said "Oldman Reilly's lawyer."

Was the body cool yet? Was the forty-dollars-an-hour meter running already? Or was it a hundred?

"What can I do for you?" I said coolly.

"Perhaps we might make an appointment to talk over . . . things?" he said.

"Perhaps we might," I said, enjoying being difficult.

Faith Christine leaned against the door with her eyebrows raised, her eyes showing amusement at my "perhaps."

"Perhaps when?" I continued.

"Are *we* going to be difficult?" he asked in a haughty voice, letting me know he was not happy with the way this little conversation was going.

"I don't know, are *we*?" I said. I was waiting to hear him say that he was "perturbed;" but he didn't. I gave him one point for that.

Faith Christine's eyebrows were telling me "Be nice."

"Shall we say tomorrow, say, at two?" Finley added.

"Yes. Say at two," I said.

"I'm next to the post office," he said. "In Rushing River Junction."

"I'll find it," I said, and hung up.

"He's not going to like you very much," she said, still looking amused and a little worried.

"He doesn't need to," I said. "I want to keep this executor thing simple."

"Do you know what an executor does here in California?" she asked.

"Yes," I said. "But I'll have to check to see if any laws have changed since I did it last. . . ."

"Before . . . say, two, tomorrow?"

"No," I said. I knew enough to get started.

I walked over and gently hugged her.

"Um, you smell good," she said. "You smell so, um, clean . . . like soap—so fresh from the shower."

"I know," I said, struggling to talk. She was hugging me back, tight. We were both feeling sad about Oldman, and perhaps worried about the danger we might both be in.

"Perhaps—" I began, determined to talk and not be reticent.

"Shut up," she said, kissing me.

Probably I'll never understand women.

Chapter Seven

"How many prospectors you got out?" I asked her. We were eating a lunch of tuna-fish sandwiches and Pepsi. We hadn't gotten around to leaving my house after the lawyer's call because I hadn't had any breakfast and realized I was hungry.

"None right this minute, John. That's why I was able to put out the CLOSED sign and come here. Been slow lately."

That mountain lion trying to chew on that jogger hadn't helped her business any. "It will pick up," I said. But that eliminated prospectors. I heard a car drive up. It was Jerry. Faith Christine made herself scarce so we could talk.

"How come you never mentioned that Mr. Oldman had a daughter last night?" Jerry said, as he walked in.

"Mostly, because I didn't know it," I said. "Faith Christine told me when I got to her house, and that was the first I knew of it."

50

We sat in my living room. I sat in my dark-green arm-chair; he sat on a couch upholstered with a color called adobe. Dora had picked it out. The couch is on the front wall under the window. My chair was near the left wall.

My house has a living room that runs front to back on the left side of the house to take advantage of the mountain views. Lots of windows. The kitchen is in the back of the house off to the right. A hallway runs down the middle of the house sideways, leading to the three bedrooms.

Jerry looked over at me and said, "This is turning out to be a strange family. Alice said she heard that Oldman's wife was strange. She was sickly all her life, and died young. Although Alice said that supposedly she and Oldman got on all right together."

"I never knew his wife. Oldman was already here when my wife and I moved here, and his wife was—I don't know—either sickly, or maybe dead, by the time I arrived. We never met her," I said.

"What about Faith Christine?"

"I don't know. You'll have to ask her."

He left me momentarily. Faith Christine had disappeared into one of the other rooms to give us privacy. Jerry walked up the hall after her.

I was still annoyed at being blamed by Jerry for not knowing about the daughter. How the heck was I supposed to know about these things?

I was annoyed at Oldman, and Jerry. Jerry had acted accusingly at me, as if I was covering up something. He's the cop; he was the one who should know things, not me.

Faith Christine came back into the living room with Jerry.

"I've only seen Oldman's wife—Jessica, I think her

name was—only once. She was a frail, sickly woman. Oldman was devoted to her, I think. I didn't know the family
well enough then to attend the funeral when she died,"
Faith Christine said.

Faith Christine and Henry had lived here about two years
longer than Dora and I.

I told Jerry about the lawyer's call.

Jerry asked Faith Christine's opinion about Oldman's
"antiques." Someone obviously had mentioned the furniture. Jerry said, "Mission-style furniture is big in New
Mexico and Arizona. My wife said so. She has relatives
down there."

Faith Christine agreed. "I was mentioning to John I think
that furniture's worth more than you might think."

"I've got to get back," Jerry said. "Let me know what
the lawyer says."

"Jerry's going to talk to Oldman's lawyer now, I bet you,
if he hasn't already," Faith Christine said, watching out the
front windows as his car disappeared from sight. "He certainly isn't giving out much information," she said.

"We're probably suspects," I said, only half-jokingly.

"That's not funny."

"I know," I said. "Sorry. Do you remember if Oldman
had any pictures—photographs—around the house of the
kids or of his wife?"

She thought for a moment, her eyebrows drawn together
a bit. "I can't remember. Let me think a minute . . . no. I
don't think so. At least, I can't think of any."

I went out to my garden to weed a little bit, and Faith
Christine watched television in the living room. Later, we
returned to her house, and she made supper. Chicken cas-
serole and salad. Apple pie.

Ken returned at dusk.

Ken and I slept over again, each taking turns again on guard.

In the morning, I went home, did my chores, and cleaned a little. Faith Christine had embarrassed me into doing it with her remarks.

Just before two o'clock I drove into Rushing River Junction. During late summer and early fall, the name could almost be taken as a joke; during spring thaws, and up until midsummer, with the snow melt coming down in a hurry off the Sierras, it could be taken as a warning about the river running west through town.

We'd had our share of people being washed away or drowned over the years, underestimating the river's power.

It was an upstairs office in a brick building. I didn't like George Finley any better in person than I did over the phone. My feeling was that Mr. Finley, Esquire (as his sign said), was going to bleed the family dry. Of what little there was.

Tiny nose, beaky chin, little black beady eyes: that was Lawyer Finley. He had a few salt-and-pepper hairs left that grew near his forehead which he left long and combed straight back; otherwise, he was pretty bald. He looked to be in his mid-sixties. Something about him made me guess that he wasn't married, but I couldn't say why I thought that. Probably divorced years ago or maybe never married. Still, he had been Oldman's lawyer for a good many years.

I had the funny feeling that he was on a fishing expedition and I didn't know why. He seemed to be pumping *me* for information on the family. He was trying to find out what I knew.

Exactly backward from what it should be.

He barely said "hi" before he began. "About Beth," he started, in a very superior tone, "what plans and arrangements did you have in mind for her?"

I lied, baldly. I play poker and I can bluff with the best of them. "The plans are still . . . well, in the planning stage," I said, mentally adding, *You son of a B.*

"And about Charles?"

"I believe he's to stay where he is at present," I said.

"Pleasant Valley Rehabilitation Center?"

"Yes," I said, having learned something. "I believe you have some papers for me?"

"Oh, yes. I was . . . expecting perhaps you might want a copy of some of these things," he said, lying. He pressed his intercom with an air of self-importance. "Miss Jacobsen, please come in here."

When his secretary came in, he gave her a stack of papers to photocopy. She stood there with them.

"I believe that is all," he said.

"I hope you've included . . ." I purposely let my voice drop and my eyebrows raise, indicating that I couldn't speak with Miss Jacobsen standing there.

He surmised that Oldman had told me something.

He looked a little annoyed and surprised, then got up reluctantly and went to a locked file cabinet, unlocked it, and pulled out a bunch of papers. He fussed over relocking it, clearly infuriated with me.

He left and came back a few minutes later, having made the photocopies himself of things he evidently did not want even Miss Jacobsen to see.

He went through the elaborate unlocking procedure again, put the original folder back in the file, relocked it, and handed me the copies, which he had taken the trouble in the outer office of putting into an expensive-looking, shiny maroon-colored pocket folder.

It probably cost him three dollars and he probably billed clients twenty dollars for it. The folder was clearly to impress them with the importance of anything coming from his office. The old snake oil salesman.

It didn't impress me.

I could tell by his expression that that was all.

"I hear that you practiced law in New York City," he said. "And that you and your wife both attended Columbia Law School," he added. "Corporate law . . . to ranching— quite a career change. I raise a few steers, myself," he said. "Black Angus." Suddenly trying to be my friend and chummy, he bumped into my elbow, he was so close as he escorted me to the door of his inner office.

I resisted the urge to verbally put this guy in his place.

"You still have a California license to practice?"

I did, although I hadn't practiced much law since I moved here twenty years ago.

I nodded.

Instead I formally shook his hand—surprised it wasn't slimy—and followed Miss Jacobsen out, where she gave me an honest, friendly smile (she didn't like him, either, I guess). She photocopied the rest of the papers for me that he had given to her in the office.

"We'll be talking soon," he ominously promised in a fakely pleasant voice as I waited with her near the very expensive copying machine, which automatically took the whole pile and was photocopying each one, one at a time. The light underneath the cover was working furiously, going back and forth.

"We need to get things squared away," he said. "I realize

you need to get all your ducks in a line first," he added, standing in his doorway with his hand on the knob. He went in and shut his inner office door, reluctantly, when he saw that I was through talking to him.

For me, it was a case of instant dislike.

When the photocopying was done, Miss Jacobsen put the papers into a manila file folder. I opened the large fancy holder Finley had given me, and closed the Velcro flap after she slid the manila folder inside. She stood straight and showed no signs of furtively peeking inside at the "secret" papers Finley had photocopied. I liked that.

"That should be interesting reading," she said, smiling, referring to the papers from the locked file.

She glanced to make sure that the door was closed tightly to Finley's inner office.

"Nice bluff you pulled in there," she said, looking me straight in the eye. "You must have been a good lawyer. If you ever decide to practice law here, call me if you need a legal secretary."

"Thank you, Miss J.," I said, shortening her name. "It has been my experience that it is much harder to fool a woman than a man."

She smiled at that. She was quite pretty.

"His ego is what trips him up," she said. "He thinks he is so superior that no one could *possibly* be fooling him."

I said a polite good-bye and left. I needed a quiet place. I went home.

Earlier, Faith Christine had mentioned that she'd be visiting Esther Cooper, the egg lady, most of the rest of the afternoon. Esther was still upset, Faith Christine said.

I pulled into my yard, went into the house, and spread

out the contents of the locked file documents first on the kitchen table.

Something that had been bothering me, that I couldn't put my fingers on, had an explanation here.

There were copies of adoption papers. Both Beth and Charles were adopted. That was not such a huge surprise, since I had recently learned that Mrs. Reilly was "sickly" all her life.

What was a surprise was that—being a somewhat cynical ex-New Yorker—I recognized poorly faked adoption papers when I saw them.

These were as fake as a gold tooth.

Nevada. The word Nevada gave me a bad feeling. Both babies were from Nevada. Any person who handles any adoption from Nevada had better be aware of Mrs. Simpson-Getts. For a period of about forty years, Mrs. Simpson-Getts had "her people"—extremely ordinary-looking men and women—steal babies from grocery stores and playgrounds in the Southern states and sell them to families here in the West, New York City, and New England. Very far away from where they had been stolen, so there would be no connection with news coverage of a missing child.

She had gotten away with it for many years. She died a natural death before ever being punished or found out.

I looked. The adoption paperwork never mentioned California. All Nevada paperwork, as if the babies were born in Nevada and went to families in Nevada. How had Simpson-Getts accomplished that?

She had an extensive underground network, as I recalled.

If Finley was in on it, he felt confident enough to give me these papers—although he had not planned on it—and

I guessed that years ago he had covered his own butt enough in some way to not worry about giving me these papers.

Maybe he simply thought I was too stupid to know it even if I saw the papers.

I didn't even know why he had these papers instead of Oldman having them. Why was that?

Jerry was still going through Oldman's papers in the desk in the back room, but it would seem that he would have mentioned that the kids were adopted. Or maybe not. Maybe Oldman didn't want any paperwork about the adoptions in his house so that the kids might inadvertently come upon them.

Did the kids know it, that they were adopted? Most kids did, these days. Supposed to be better, psychologically, to tell them right off, when they were little.

But that was not as strongly felt thirty years ago. Adoptions were more secretive. Some parents never told children they were adopted back then.

There were a lot of other papers, mostly dealing with Beth's troubles—they seemed serious—but there was nothing specific about what the problem was. Some papers were about Charles.

Bad grades, stuff like that. Warnings from teachers, bad report cards. Why did the lawyer have all these things? Why not Oldman? What the devil was going on here?

Was Oldman scared of his kids?

Chapter Eight

"Do you want to go, or not?" I asked Faith Christine that evening at her house. I was sitting at the table while she was cooking supper.

Ken was back again. He was outside; he said he had eaten earlier.

"I don't know," she said, sliding a spatula under the pancake, and then deciding to let it cook some more before she turned it over. She pulled out the spatula. "I don't know."

The small pile of bacon, already cooked and on a platter on the table, made the kitchen smell great. There was a big bowl of homemade applesauce next to it.

She turned and looked at me. She had on a pretty blue blouse and jeans, and her hair looked all soft and fluffy. She even had on a little lipstick. "I remember Beth as being a little weird. I don't know if she ever liked me, or would even talk to me, if I went."

"She's spent a lot of time in institutions," I said. "That has to be rough."

We were discussing whether we should start contacting and/or going to nearby psychiatric institutions to try to locate Beth. And whether I should go alone or if Faith Christine should come with me.

I was sitting there speculating whether Beth's emotional troubles began with the trauma of being kidnapped, when the doorbell rang.

"Who is that?" I asked.

"How would I know?" Faith Christine laughed. "Go look and see."

I peered out through the blue-and-white checkered-pattern living room curtains before I opened the door. "It's some teenage kid," I said.

I opened the door.

"What can I do for you?" I said to the black-haired kid who stood there. Or, it would have been black if there had been any—I was going strictly by root color through the shave.

Faith Christine brushed by me and grabbed the kid and hugged him.

"Charles," she said, pointedly.

"Charles," I said. "Come on in."

His hands were evidently sweaty because he wiped them on his faded jeans before he shook, rather formally, my hand. Up close I could see that he was a lot older, not a teenager as I had first imagined. He just was dressed like one.

"Sorry," I said. "About your father."

He nodded.

"Here," I said. "Sit." I indicated the couch.

He didn't.

He stood, rocking back a little on one foot, and twisting his other leg just enough to stand there looking awkward.

So was I. Feeling awkward.

What did I say next? How is rehab?

"How is rehab?" Faith Christine asked.

"Fine," he said.

He looked at me. There was a silence.

"I hear you are in charge of . . . everything."

"Not everything."

"I guess that my father didn't trust me," he said.

"We don't know that," I said. "Maybe he thought that your plate was rather full right now." That sounded stupid, even to me. Oldman didn't know he was going to die right that day . . . or did he? Oddly, that seemed to appease Charles. His face relaxed, somewhat.

"Coffee?" Faith Christine said.

He nodded yes, and when we sat at the table, without asking, she brought him a huge pile of pancakes which he began to devour, along with bacon and the coffee, as if he was starving. He was so skinny, maybe he was, for all I knew.

He didn't look dangerous, just lost, and kind of sad. I handed him the applesauce, and he scooped out some. If what I thought had happened to him had really happened, he'd had a tough life.

Did he have a clue he might have been a stolen baby? Could I, should I bring it up? Was this a bad time? What did he know? How fragile was he emotionally? Why was he out of rehab today? You weren't supposed to leave, were you? Then again, his father had just been murdered. That probably took precedence, even in a rehab situation.

"Oh, great!" he said, suddenly. "I left my counselor, Miss Whitaker, out in the car!" He jumped up and ran out, returning and knocking on the door with a woman who looked very youthful—evidently Miss Whitaker.

That explained a few things. She seemed like a nice young woman, not lacking in self-confidence, certainly. Tiny nose, white, white skin. Normal hair on her head. Brown. Long and straight. Green eyes. Probably weighed a tad over a hundred pounds. Had a white blouse and a black skirt on. Looked businesslike, professional.

Faith Christine handed her coffee, pancakes, applesauce, and bacon. Miss Whitaker politely refused the bacon, indicating without actually mentioning it that she was a vegetarian. Ate the applesauce and pushed the pancake around the plate, pretending to eat it.

Charles. The fake birth certificate said he was twenty-eight. A *lot* older than a teenager.

Beth would be thirty. I couldn't believe that I had seen them so rarely. Beth I could understand; she had been gone from here most of her life. But why hadn't I seen Charles more? Where had he been?

More likely, I had seen him but he looked a lot different than he did now. He probably had hair on his head. People look remarkably alike to me with their heads shaved bald. It makes their facial characteristics less noticeable, at least to me. Maybe that's why they do it. Or maybe it's just that you are staring at their scalp as their most noticeable feature and not looking at much else.

And the three gold rings piercing his left eyebrow might have confused me some.

I'll have to ask Faith Christine what she thinks about the subject sometime, I thought to myself.

These things tend to be a mystery to me. Anyway, Faith Christine seemed to know him well enough, and was appearing to be comfortable with them both. She drew Miss Whitaker off, after they finished eating, into the living room. I heard them discussing vegetarian recipes.

I knew she was doing that so I could talk to the boy— no, the man. I had to admit that Charles was, in age, a man, although my gut feeling was that, realistically, he was very immature. Shockingly so for his age. He looked both vulnerable and helpless.

"Tell me about yourself," I started, figuring I needed to know what he knew.

"Not much to tell," he said.

At least he didn't say "Ain't much to tell."

"Heard you were the guy who organized the teenage rodeo for the high school kids," he said. "That was cool," he said. "Went a couple of times."

"We had a lot of fun," I said. "How much longer do you need to stay in rehab?" I asked.

"Depends on money," he said bluntly. "She"—he nodded his shaved head toward the living room—"says I should stay another month—at least four more weeks." He looked at me. "But I don't know what happens now."

"Tell her that you can stay where you are, as long as you need to. In fact, I'll tell her. I'll see she gets paid."

"What about the funeral?"

"Leave me your number. I'll let you know when the body is released by the police."

"From doing the autopsy?"

"Basically."

"I can't make arrangements very well from Los Angeles."

"If it's all right, I think Faith Christine will—wants to take care of that. Tell her if there's anything special you want done."

"Thank you, Mr. Ranger. You and Mrs. Butler are great."

He paused for a moment. "If you ever need help with the rodeo . . ."

I smiled. "I don't do that anymore. But I'll keep you in mind."

Faith Christine came back in with Miss Whitaker. I suspected that they had been listening as well as talking, as women sometimes do. Miss Whitaker spoke first. "It's a long drive, but we'll be back for the funeral. Everything all set with him staying, then, at Pleasant Valley?"

"Yup," I said, shaking Charles's hand. "All set for now."

Miss Whitaker gave me two phone numbers for Pleasant Valley. One for her, one for him.

Shortly after, they left.

"Darn it," I said. "I forgot to ask him about Beth."

"Not to worry," Faith Christine said. "I asked her."

"Well?"

"He doesn't know where she is. They haven't spoken in two years. Some kind of fight or something."

"Great," I said.

"What about the papers from the lawyer? Surely, the lawyer's been paying Beth's bills and stuff all these years?"

"Apparently not. At least, not since two years ago. And there's no mention of where Beth is now in the paperwork he gave me."

"The lack of bills means that she's probably out."

"Not necessarily. Don't forget she's thirty. She's an adult

now. One, she might be out of state; two, she might be in an institution as a ward of the state anywhere in the U. S.; three—" I shook my head.

"There could be a thousand reasons and a thousand places—I get the picture. She could be married—or dead," she said. "You'll have to ask him. You'll have to ask George Finley."

I groaned. He'd have caught me bluffing.

Still, he had asked about my "plans and arrangements" for Beth. That indicated that he thought that something needed to be done. But what?

"Not one of your favorite people?"

"No."

"Miss Whitaker looks frighteningly young for such responsibility . . . and it doesn't seem to bother her one bit," Faith Christine said.

"I guess it's just us Stone Age folks who worry," I said, jokingly.

"Well, if she worries, she sure doesn't show it."

"Vegetarians always know everything," I said.

"You male vegetationist pig," she said, hugging me.

Chapter Nine

If Jerry had any sense, he should be checking on the whereabouts, rumors, and activities of all the people involved in the mining fiasco, I thought grumpily as I got into my own bed later. They had motive, as they say, and opportunity.

I was sure he was doing that. He didn't seem stupid.

It had been a long day. After visiting the lawyer, George Finley, and before going to supper at Faith Christine's, I had spent the later part of the afternoon doing as many of the things as I could for Oldman's estate. Routine paperwork for a death.

Notifying people, institutions, and agencies. He wouldn't be needing his driver's license, for instance.

Some things I couldn't do yet. I had decided to leave the phone on for a few days at Oldman's house.

I was back at my own house because I had things to do.

I had taken care of my daily chores and taken care of the livestock.

Ken seemed to have gotten the hang of being more careful.

I had called my son, who was a computer nut and had computer nut friends, and they were looking into the whereabouts of Beth Reilly. They wanted to know if her name was really Elizabeth, but as far as I knew, no, it wasn't. Her fake birth certificate said Beth.

My son Peter had said, "Dad, do you have any idea how many Elizabeth Reillys there are in America?"

We both agreed that the name Beth might cut it down some.

Man, I was tired.

Faith Christine called. The phone was next to my bed.

"I just want to tell you that an adult, rugged-looking cop named Richard Brown is giving Ken a break, and he's guarding me until Ken comes back on duty in the morning."

I was relieved. We said good-bye and hung up.

I closed my eyes, marveling at how comfortable the bed was. My head was nestled in my pillow like it was a nest.

The phone rang again.

It was Jerry.

"We just found George Finley."

"So?"

"Dead in his office."

I sat up.

"Knife wounds?"

"Seventeen or eighteen."

"Great."

"Heard you were at the office today."

"Yes. At two."

I thought. "Any on his hands, like at Oldman's?"

"Yes."

"I don't suppose—" I said.

"Yes. I was wondering if you could . . ."

Inwardly, I groaned.

I arrived twenty minutes later, and went through my now-familiar routine with the plastic gloves and booties.

"One of our guys happened to come by and saw that a light was still on in Finley's office. He called me, and I went to investigate. Lucky I did."

George Finley had over-billed his last client.

As I looked, Jerry said, "Blood was found in the drains at Reilly's. Someone cleaned up before they left the scene. No bloody clothing, though. Must have put it in something and carried it away."

I assumed that that meant the police were checking all the trash and garbage containers all around the area near Oldman's, and every place where a fire had been lit.

"Jerry, do you know where Beth Reilly is?" I asked.

"Not yet. Poor kid has been through the mill, here and there, shuffled from place to place over the years. I have a list in my office. But the trail, as it were, ends two years ago, when they let her out of Tranquility House. There was a rumor that she was in a homeless shelter in San Francisco. We're checking. I asked around the best I could. Town gossip is that it was weird; neither kid looked like Oldman. Must have taken after the mother."

"They were adopted," I said. "You're going to find out when you go through the papers in that locked file over there," I said, indicating the filing cabinet in back of the desk.

To do this I had to look past the bloody body of George Finley, who was sitting in the chair at his desk, thoroughly dead. That caught my attention. His head hung back over the chair, his mouth open.

It was then that I noticed that the same drawer in the file cabinet was open just a bit, the file that had been so carefully locked by Finley on my first visit here today.

"Rats," I said. "That file was locked earlier. I thought that file might give us additional information either about Beth or Oldman."

Jerry walked carefully around and opened the filing cabinet. "There's a big chunk of files missing from this drawer," he said. "The front of the file"—he bent to look at the label on the front of the drawer—"says M TO S. Inside, only S is left. First name in here is Shockley: Shockley, Ruth R. Everything else is gone."

Great.

"Either there was no time to take just what was necessary so they grabbed a lot of files, or there was something in other files in there of importance," he said.

"I wonder if the murderer or murderers knew that Finley had given me copies of some of the documents in that file." I said. "We need to talk to Miss Jacobsen."

From the look on his face I knew the answer before he said it.

"She's disappeared," he said.

"That's the reason you wanted me here," I said.

"You talked with her today," he said.

I don't read cops' minds, but our guess had been that Jerry was going to go to talk to the lawyer next when he left Faith Christine and me. Obviously, he hadn't. I'm sure he had a load of cop things to do; maybe he was busy with something else more pressing about the murder. I just wished he had. So did he, was my guess. Probably feeling remorse. After I was through at Finley's, I went to sit in my truck and think for a minute. I let my mind run away with me and pictured Miss Jacobsen's body somewhere in a field or on a mountain, dead.

Then I realized—remembered—that she was one smart cookie, and if she sensed that the poop was heading toward the fan, she just might have run away somewhere smart and fast—and gotten away.

The question was, was she hiding somewhere? And was she somewhere where I could find her?

And if I did find her, would I put her in danger? What if she didn't know anything, anyway? Was I being followed and too stupid to realize it? I'd watch my back from now on.

If she didn't know anything, maybe she wouldn't have needed to run. Or maybe the murderer or murderers didn't know if she knew anything or not.

It was very late when I reached home. Peter, my son, would have a Miss Jacobsen added to his computer search list. I needed her first name. As kids would say, "Duh." I found her first name by looking in the local phone book. Fifteen minutes later, I had Peter on the phone, and he agreed to begin looking for Patricia Jacobsen. In particular, any relatives she might have nearby.

His return call came fifteen minutes later. Miss J. had three relatives living close by.

"I didn't need the computer, Dad," he said. "I just called a friend from high school and asked about the family."

I wrote the names down as he spoke.

"So far I haven't had any luck locating Beth Reilly," he

said. To his credit, he never said a word about his dad calling him at two in the morning. Or what his friend said, getting a phone call from Peter at that hour.

I got into my bed for the second time that night.

Should I call the people? No. That would be stupid. I was going to have to find each relative and visit them personally. But not tonight. Tomorrow morning. Which was only a couple of hours away.

I slept.

Chapter Ten

In the morning when I arrived, Faith Christine was busy on the phone making the arrangements for Oldman's funeral. Ken would be with her, at least for today. As with anybody who hung around her long, they were getting to be quite chummy, and from the way they talked to each other, I knew he had told her of his romantic troubles and his whole life story, besides.

Meanwhile, Oldman's body was due to be released soon. Either late today or early tomorrow, and the funeral was tentatively scheduled for the day after that, at nine-thirty in the morning. She had called Charles and told him this. She said she'd call him back if there was any change.

He seemed to be doing okay.

I went back home and did some letter writing and made some more calls having to do with Oldman's estate.

Peter and Jerry were both still working, in their own

ways, on locating Beth. Jerry wanted her for questioning, and I wanted her for the funeral—if she wanted to come. I felt I at least owed her notification of her father's death.

Did she read newspapers at all? What to do next? Let the adoption thing go for now, and put Miss Jacobsen top priority? Sounded like a good idea. But maybe a five-minute phone call wouldn't hurt. Information, first, to get the number of the *Nevada Morning Register,* the paper that I remembered from my New York days had broken the story of the Nevada adoption scandal. After dialing the number, I asked to speak to the head of the newsroom.

After I explained what I wanted, I was passed from person to person at the paper, department to department, and I watched as the clock inched forward. Feeling guilty that I had made a bad decision. Losing time that I should be using to find Patricia Jacobsen. Stress. Once I was totally disconnected and had to dial again. But now I—stubbornly—didn't want to give up after wasting this much time already. I could feel myself losing patience. Finally I got a man named Eddie Something. He said that Bob Harris, who had broken the story, was "No longer with the paper."

"May I ask the reason?"

"Deceased."

For a moment my heart pumped faster, and I asked, "Do you mind telling me what was the cause of death?"

Eddie said, "It was a long battle with lung cancer. Bob was a notoriously heavy smoker. Two packs a day."

It would not be a lie to say that sorry as I was, I was also relieved. Chatting some more, loosening him up, I sucked the information out of Eddie that he and Bob were drinking (and smoking) buddies after business hours, and he was still grieving over his loss, which was two months ago.

Shamelessly using this, I managed to get the information out of Eddie that Mrs. Simpson-Getts managed to achieve the adoptions so furtively and cleverly that problems with the state of Nevada—or any other state—had never surfaced. The woman was an evil criminal genius at manipulating the whole U.S. interstate legal system to her advantage.

It was only when the stolen children reached their thirties that some of them had flashbacks. Memories that were able to be traced back and verified as true specific names and places—finally brought the ring's activities out into the open. One kid, now an adult man living on his own in southern California, kept flashing back to a street in New Orleans, that, as far as he knew, he had never been to.

He remembered the colors of houses and street names and details of how the streetlights looked. He remembered the name of a bakery that smelled of bread, and the name of a fish market that smelled of fish on that street. He could see the street very clearly in his mind, even so far as remembering where storm drains were located. When the man flew down from Nevada and checked, he was astounded to find out his recollections were totally accurate.

Then he found out that a child who lived on that same street had been abducted and never found. It was a famous case, never solved. The description of the child matched the man's eye and hair color and recollections. Worse, the date of the kidnapping and the ages of how old he was and how old the snatched child would be now, matched. It was very traumatic. And later, his DNA was a match with his New Orleans biological parents.

When he went back home and confronted his adoptive parents, he was horrified to learn that his parents had illegally "purchased" him when he was two and a half years old from Mrs. Simpson-Getts.

"It was very hard for him to forgive his adopted parents," Eddie said. "That one case was what brought the baby-stealing ring out into the open. No one was ever prosecuted. Because Simpson-Getts had lived for the last twenty-five years in Nevada, Bob Harris covered the case for the paper. It was a big story. National coverage."

He continued, "DNA tests were able to positively identify and reunite about ten or twelve of the now-adult children and their parents. But unless they have a flashback, there's no way of locating most of the children. No truthful paperwork trail. Nevada authorities figure there are about eighty more 'lost' stolen children—now adults—floating around the United States," he added. "The records are useless because they were a mass of lies. Fake names of birth parents, fake birth certificates, and so forth. A paperwork nightmare, even for experts. She fit the description 'evil genius' to a T."

No wonder Oldman had chosen this isolated rural area to live. Dang! I hate it when people have a bad reason for doing such a nice thing as moving here. Isolation and privacy. Hiding out with stolen children. It made me angry. How can people like that live with themselves? Selfishness, I guess. Was it something to do with the stolen children that had caused Oldman's death?

I hung up. Next, I had to try to locate Patricia Jacobsen. I hoped she wasn't in danger from this mess. And now I was late starting to look for her relatives and friends this morning. Still, I was grateful to Eddie for having been such help, when he didn't have to be.

I got in my truck and turned left out of my driveway, toward Rushing River Junction. Patricia's aunt, Mrs. Austin Singer, lived on Sunnydale Road. As I pulled up to park in her driveway, the door to the yellow thirties-style house opened and a magnificent brown-and-black Great Dane came out barking. If Miss J. was here, it bode well for her safety. I rolled down the window and said as much to the dyed-too-black–haired lady with the pleasant face who followed the big brown dog out of the house.

The dog never took his eyes off me, alert, muscles tensed and standing guard, in case I planned on opening the truck door and stepping down onto his territory. He acted like I was Al Capone and he was J. Edgar Hoover.

He needn't have worried. That truck door was staying closed. Locked, even. I only opened the window a small bit; noting how much space that dog's mouth would take to fill up the open window space. I told her who I was, and asked her to get in touch with me, after contacting Miss Jacobsen, if she knew where she was.

I wrote my number on a piece of paper, after thinking a minute, and deciding against adding the phone number at Faith Christine's. I trusted nobody, at this point.

I never got out of my truck to further disturb the dog, who was still not trusting me even though the woman was talking to me. Although dogs generally like me, and I have never been bitten by a dog. I certainly didn't want to break my perfect record by taking a chance with this seventy-pounder. I simply handed Mrs. Singer the paper with my phone number on it out of the truck window.

I was pretty much sure that Mrs. Austin Singer knew

where Patricia was, and I was pretty sure that she wasn't at this house. I could tell by how relaxed the woman was; she was not glancing back at the house in a protective way, checking the windows to see if anyone was peeking out.

After assuring her who I was ("a friendly"), I finished by saying that she was to remind Miss Jacobsen that she had offered to work for me in the future, something only she and I would know.

The woman was understandably closed-mouthed about the whereabouts of Patricia, and I drove off, toward the next name on the list that Peter had given me over the phone: Arlene Jacobsen. Work: Jones Insurance Agency. I knew where that was—a short distance from George Finley's office.

She'd be at work now. I drove there, parked, and went in the tiny storefront on Main Street, three doors down from the post office, near Finley's law office.

The windows needed washing, and the place was rather dingy. Not doing a fabulous business, I guessed. Three big old-fashioned oak desks, jammed into a small space. Putty-colored metal file cabinets along the walls, with chipped paint and dings. Skinny old brick building. Cheap rent.

Two desks with signs of active use; Arlene's and one other, probably used by the owner, Mr. Jones, lined up together in the front. There was only a small space between the desks, barely enough to make a passway to the back room.

There she was, sitting at one of the two front desks, the one on the right. She didn't look busy. She stood up when she saw me come in.

Arlene Jacobsen, Patricia's sister, reminded me of her in

that she looked you directly in the eye, and was of similar height and weight, and maybe a smidge less good-looking.

I wondered idly if Peter would like either of these fine young women. He was always complaining that the women in Los Angeles were too interested in your assets rather than your character: "Your Porsche, not your principles," was how he put it.

I told him, "Then don't drive one."

Pig-headed (I wonder where he gets it), he says, "Why should I give up driving something I like?"

I had to remind myself at times like that, that my parenting job is done; they are on their own now to learn things. I don't give advice unless they ask for it specifically. Anyway, I right away decided to do a bit of introducing, if Peter came up for the funeral. It couldn't hurt. It couldn't hurt that my mother's name was Arlene.

I smiled my most devious, charming (I hoped) smile at her; visualizing grandchildren that looked like her or her sister. Dark hair and eyes, nice pleasant faces, and lovely skin. Standing, Arlene was about five feet six, maybe an inch taller than Patricia. I smiled, hoping that if I was charming enough, she would tell me where her sister was.

She laughed and said, "I think I know you. You ran the rodeo for the high school kids, didn't you?"

She came around the desk and continued, "I didn't ride, but I used to come and hang over the fence and watch practice," she said. "And I know Peter."

She finished off by saying, "Haven't seen him since high school. He was a nice kid."

"He's not married," I said, probably too obviously. I added, "He might be up for the funeral."

"Cool," she said.

"Have you seen your sister?" She laughed again.

"No. But she called me. Said my aunt called her and said you were just there. How'd you like Thor?"

"The Great Dane?"

"Yes. You get out of the car?"

"No. I stayed in my truck. I'm no fool," I said, chuckling. I was still trying to charm her.

"He's a nice dog. But if he senses fear, he bites that person—nips that person—right in the rear."

"I like a dog with a sense of humor," I said.

"So do I."

"Patricia, come on out. This one doesn't bite," she unexpectedly called out. She turned and looked toward the dark-paneled wooden door at the back of the office.

Patricia opened the door just a crack, and peeked out.

"I lied," Arlene said. "She's here."

Patricia Jacobsen looked scared. She was taking this a lot more seriously than her sister was. She didn't come out but used her hand to beckon me to come in the back room.

I did. "What happened?" I said, as I closed the door behind me. There was a brown vinyl couch with a pale pink blanket folded neatly on it. Didn't look too comfortable. It was a room mostly used for storage. The shades were pulled down. The room smelled of stirred-up dust.

"Arlene's insurance office was open till eight because they were expecting a customer at seven-thirty, and I came here. I slept here last night." She glanced toward the couch unhappily.

"What exactly happened—what was going on? What happened to George Finley?" I asked.

Nobody sat.

"Do you know about the adoptions?" she asked.

"Yes. Fake paperwork."

She surprised me when she said, "George was not in on that, as far as I know. Even though he was Oldman's lawyer for a long time."

We heard the phone ring in the outer office.

"He never did anything about it, even though he knew," I said, trying to keep the bitterness out of my voice.

"No. I don't know why—maybe he liked Oldman, maybe it was lawyer-client privilege."

I shook my head in disgust.

"Maybe Oldman was paying him to keep quiet?" she said.

"There's a terrible lack of ethics there," I said. "Baby stealing." I said, my anger building up. "He should have done something. He could have done it in an anonymous way. Especially if he knew for years and years."

She shook her head in agreement.

"How did you find out?" I asked. "How long have you known?"

"Yesterday. Something was happening yesterday. George was acting stressed out, worried about something after you left. About three-thirty I had run out for five minutes—to buy a can of coffee for the office at the market—and when I walked into my office, George—this is . . . was very unlike him—had his door open and was arguing with someone on the phone."

"Who?"

"I couldn't tell."

"Man or woman?"

"Couldn't tell. Someone must have said something because I heard him say in an angry voice, 'No, you're not! Not one more!'—real loud. Then he noticed the door was open, and that I was back. He put down the phone and came over and slammed the door shut. Hard. I left at six o'clock, and when I heard that he had been killed—one of my friends called me—I came here to hide."

Arlene, who had quietly entered as Patricia talked, closed the door softly behind her, her smile gone.

"It's all right. My boss, Mr. Jones, is a nice guy. He knows she's here. But he wants her to leave and go and see Jerry Vivens soon—in fact, she should as soon as she finishes talking to you. My aunt says she talked to somebody who knows you and they said you were a big lawyer in New York City."

"Corporate law," I said. "Mergers. And that was years and years ago."

"Oh," Patricia said, her face showing disappointment. "Am I wrong to hide?" she said anxiously. "Am I in danger?"

"I don't know," I said. "To tell the truth, I don't know what the heck is going on."

I frowned. "Is there anything else you can think of, that you should tell me? Is there anything else you know—that you think I should know?"

"About the office?"

"About the office, about George, about anything."

She shook her head. "There was a whole file drawer of files that he kept locked, that he'd never let *anybody* see."

"Anything else?"

She shook her head again.

"Whoever killed Finley might not know that. I think we should call Jerry, and have him come over here and pick you up. His office is just two blocks away. He's looking for you. We all thought that maybe something had happened to you. We've been very worried. After you talk to him we can decide what to do, if you want."

Should she join the group at Faith Christine's, or stay at the house with the Great Dane guard dog?

We'd have to wait and decide that later.

Maybe Jerry had some suggestions.

Chapter Eleven

We called Jerry and I waited for him to arrive. It was decided he would drop her off at Faith Christine's when the police were done questioning her. Jerry called Faith Christine from the insurance office and asked her if Patricia was welcome at the ranch. She was.

"I'll stay at Faith Christine's with them and Ken as a precaution, but I want to go home first and see if there are any messages on my answering machine from Peter," I told Jerry. "Peter's looking for Beth on the Internet."

I left and drove off. Peter was known jokingly in my family as "Even Peter." Peter was the most like Dora of our three children—tall, smart, blond.

He was involved with electronics stuff and computers from an early age. He was smart, smarter than me. Almost as smart as Dora. He was good at fixing things, even I had to admit. However, he was a difficult child to please, and our family over the years had begun saying things like "The birthday cake was good—even Peter liked it," or "The cat was sick—even Peter was concerned."

I was wondering if Peter would like either Arlene or Patricia romantically, because even Peter would have to admit that a person's character was more important to these girls than a Porsche—or they wouldn't be living here in a small town whose prominent feature was dirt and plenty of it.

I knew that Faith Christine would scold me and tell me that I didn't even know if Patricia and Arlene were unattached—it was just like her to be practical like that. The thought crossed my mind that you're pretty much committed to a woman when everything that happens, you run through your mind what you think she's going to have to say about it.

I drove home, looking to see if anyone was following me. It didn't appear so. I went directly to the barn, did my chores, and checked on the cattle before I entered the house.

No message from Peter, so I left him one on his machine, mentioning Arlene remembering him, telling him about finding Patricia, and about George Finley's death.

I scrambled myself an egg and buttered some toast and ate. After I cleaned up the kitchen, I went to sit in my armchair. One, where was Beth? Could I find her? Who killed Oldman—and why? Who killed George Finley—and why? Was it connected to the mining thing? Or was it connected to the adoption thing?

In a way, we were stumped until we located Beth. She was the key, even if just to eliminate some theories. I needed a picture of her.

The California Department of Motor Vehicles could do a photo match on her license picture through the police department—if she had a license under the name Beth Reilly. Peter would have checked that instantly.

What if she didn't drive? Darn! I should have asked Charles if he had a photo of her. What if she had gotten married? Peter must be checking on that. *Peter, call me,* I thought, and the phone rang.

It was Jerry.

Oh, no!

"No, no . . . it's not what you think," he said quickly. "I know what happened the last two times I called, but this time . . ." he said. The line was silent for a moment.

"Are you grouchy, John?"

"I'm not in a good mood, that's true," I said. "Did you get anything helpful from Miss Jacobsen?"

"Not really," he said. "I just have a few more questions, but we're taking a coffee break."

He was quiet for a moment.

"I'm in way over my head here, John."

"I understand that. I feel the same way."

"I want to find Reilly's and Finley's killer or killers. People are beginning to panic—to freak out. Nobody expects murders to happen here. Now we've had two."

"I know."

"You have a reputation for being smart."

"That's false. Entirely false."

"Faith Christine says so."

"What does that have to do with anything?"

"If she thinks you're smart, I do, too."

Faith Christine again. I pictured how pretty she was looking lately.

"I got some information a little while ago. Andrew Smith, one of the higher-up guys in the mining scheme. He committed suicide a few days ago in New York City," Jerry said. "He was some kind of genius and he had a history of depression." Then he added, "His even more troubled brother, Thomas, has disappeared. Police in the NYPD called and suggested that he might come out here and try to exact revenge. Said it is a *remote* possibility, but is a possibility. He's an average-looking guy, five-eight or so, with a small scar on his chin."

"I'll tell everyone involved to be on the lookout." I knew Jerry. I knew there was something else. "What do you want, Jerry?" I said, giving up.

"Can I come over later this afternoon? Don't worry, this time I'm not asking you to come to me . . . I'll bring what information I have, and we can compare notes. I mean, after I finish up here and drop Miss Jacobsen off at Faith Christine's."

"Of course," I said, and hung up.

I looked out the window. Gray Mist was living up to its name. The sky was overcast. I called Faith Christine and warned her about Thomas Smith.

Then I stood there looking for a few minutes, sighed a few times, and went in to the bathroom to wash up and shave, something that I hadn't had a chance to do yet today.

As I dragged the razor over the shaving cream I thought about crime . . . and good and evil. Abelard said that men are free to choose between good and evil.

St. Thomas Aquinas, whom I tend to agree with on most things, said that man bears the responsibility for good and evil, not God. God just gives you choices. Did God forget how stupid and evil people can be?

I sighed again as I tapped the razor on the sink to remove the cut stubble, and then I finished shaving under my jaw. Dora never liked it when I left a messy sink.

Walking into the living room, I sat in my favorite green chair and waited for Jerry. The doorbell rang.

Jerry looked awful, as did I.

"Hi, Jerry. You look like something the cat dragged in," I said, grasping his outstretched hand and shaking it.

"Ditto," he said, looking back at me. I chuckled, and let go of his hand. I stepped back to allow him to come further into the house. "I was up late last night," he said. "Again."

He probably would be until these two murders were solved. Walking together to the kitchen, I got out two large mugs. He sat at the kitchen table.

"Do you mind decaf?" I asked. "I can make regular if you want."

"Decaf's fine. Stomach gets funny if I drink too much regular these days. Doesn't keep me awake at night, though. At this point, I don't think the noise from a 747 jet airliner would keep me awake, even if it was coming in for a landing in my front yard."

"Wait till you're my age," I said. "Regular keeps you up all night, worrying about what mistakes you made twenty years ago. A list of your imperfections marches before your sleepless eyes. Things like, were you mean to your college roommate thirty years ago?"

"Whoa. Don't let me get that old," Jerry said.

"How old are you?" I asked.

"Thirty-eight."

"A mere baby," I said. "Wait till you turn fifty. I hated it when I turned fifty."

"When was that?" Jerry asked.

"Two months ago. I still hate being fifty."

"Helene and I moved up here five years ago to get away from the crime. We have two girls and didn't want them growing up in a high-crime area. Crime seems to have followed us here." I knew he and Helene had moved here from a suburb of Los Angeles.

I got out milk and sugar and two spoons. We got down to business. Jerry had a notebook with him, the kind that you flip the pages over to get to the next page.

He read from his notes as I poured the coffee. "Tea was in Oldman's stomach, the report said."

Tea was in Oldman's stomach? I didn't think that news was helpful, particularly.

"The thing that interests me was the stab wounds on the hands," I said. "They seemed to me—and I am no expert— that they were direct stabs in his hands, like 'Keep your hands off me,' or 'Keep your hands off my business,' kinds of wounds. Like after he was already down. Punishment stabs."

Jerry made a face. "I disagree. To me they looked like stabs received from fighting off the killer."

Neither one of us really knew what we were talking about. But he was probably right.

"Have you done anything yet as Oldman's administrator?" Jerry asked, taking a drink of his coffee.

"I'm not his administrator," I said. "I'm the executor. There's a difference. Almost always, a will names someone to be the executor. If there's no will, the court appoints someone who is called the administrator of the estate.

"The executor carries out the terms of the will, while the administrator—because there is no will—carries out the laws of the state," I finished.

"So things, in effect, could be different, depending on whether there is an administrator or executor," Jerry said.

"Yes. Very. I'm an executor. I need to see that the terms of the will are carried out," I said.

"Oh, boy," Jerry said.

"What?" I asked.

"Oh, no."

"What do you mean?"

"Didn't George Finley give you the papers about Jessica's—Oldman's wife's—estate?"

"No. Mostly about the kids and their adoption, and a few legal papers on unimportant things. And it certainly appeared that Oldman didn't have any money from the papers I received. I think maybe he might have a couple of thousand in the bank, his ratty old truck, and his house."

We both knew that Oldman was a retired carpenter—which you never could have told by looking at his house.

I didn't have to add that his house needed a lot of work.

"That slimeball," Jerry said, feelingly.

I didn't know which man he was referring to.

Things suddenly became a lot clearer when he said, "George Finley, Esquire, was the executor of Jessica Shaw Reilly's estate—worth millions. Old money. Her family has been in California since the Gold Rush. Quietly got rich opening a chain of dry goods stores. Her maiden name was Shaw."

"That explains why the first file left in the filing cabinet was Sho . . . Shockley. It probably was next after the Shaw file," I said. "Somebody grabbed the Shaw files, along with the Reilly files."

No wonder Charles didn't ask whether there was enough *money* for him to stay . . . only *if* he could stay.

And it answered one of the questions that had been bothering me: where would Oldman and Jessica have gotten all the money to pay for the two stolen babies? Stolen babies are never cheap. Even for that time, back then. Jessica or Jessica's family had probably paid. He and his wife must have paid big bucks for the stolen children.

But why was Oldman living like that the last twenty years? As if he was almost destitute. Penance? Guilt?

Had it been mostly Jessica's idea or pushing that had driven him to be a party to stealing babies? Sometimes chronically ill people can be very manipulative and forceful, learning early how to get their own way. And she or her family must have controlled the purse strings.

Was Jessica's will specific about leaving nothing to Oldman—just the kids? I could understand that, in a way. Given the history of the children's problems. And that I had a feeling that she was not a very nice woman to start with.

Oldman was a self-sufficient person; at least I had judged him to be . . . yet the mining company would have been able to pull the wool over his eyes if I hadn't stopped by to talk. Did he have a history of being manipulated?

Why hadn't George Finley told me what was really going on? With Oldman's death, was he going to take Jessica Shaw's money and run? Abandon his tiny upstairs office and head for the Bahamas? It wouldn't have been the first time a lawyer did that.

Surely he would have known that I'd find out through a paperwork trail about Jessica's will. Was he planning to be long gone by then? Before his theft was discovered? He was a fool if he didn't think I'd find out eventually, either from the newspapers or at the courthouse. Well, he *was* a fool. Probably a greedy fool. Or maybe he was covering up his own crimes. Embezzlement? It seemed likely. When—if—papers were found, we'd probably find that he'd been bleeding the estate dry over the years.

That wouldn't surprise me. Billing the estate for bogus hours and fees for this and that. California has decent laws to prevent that but crooks always find ways.

My guess he was guilty of something or he would have mentioned Jessica's will to me. He was probably a crook. Giving himself more time. Had he killed Oldman? That thought came and went quickly when I remembered the stab wounds on both sets of hands.

Keep your hands off my money?

I remembered Jerry's assumption, and realized that he'd been sitting there an awful long time waiting for an answer to his question.

"Sorry, Jerry. I was thinking. No, Finley and I would both be executors. So nothing basically would be changed, as far as that goes."

"Except with Oldman dead and Finley dead, everything *is* changed," he said.

"That's true. And, as we don't know what the heck has been going on with Jessica's estate, we won't know until we find out. He must have left a paper trail somewhere."

"IRS?"

I groaned.

"Now I'm responsible for unpaid back taxes. Thanks, Oldman," I said bitterly, assuming that Finley hadn't paid taxes on Jessica's estate, which would now fall to Oldman's heirs' estate to settle.

"What exactly are you responsible for as executor?"

"A lot of things. Getting copies of his death certificate

to banks, post offices, insurers; getting court permission to gain access to the will, if it is in a safe deposit box; finding and paying a tax accountant; notifying Social Security; the Veterans Administration, if he was a vet; contacting his pension plan if there is any; gathering bank and brokerage statements from three previous years, making a preliminary estimate of the value of real estate and personal property, and of the estate's total value—"

"Give money to the kids?"

"Yes. And make any payments to avoid default, collect life insurance payments, make sure present fire and home and property insurance is adequate, register the will—apply to Probate Court—compile a list of assets and property for the court, obtain appraisals if necessary, record every expenditure, pay creditors, put legal notices in newspapers." And the right of first refusal which might or might not apply . . . I didn't bring that up.

"Sorry I asked," Jerry said, noting the increasing annoyance in my voice as I spoke.

"The laws vary a little from state to state," I said, looking at him. "I'm not angry at you. I left New York years ago to get away from things like that. I hired a lawyer as executor of my wife's estate, although most of our stuff was survivorship and fairly simple."

"It's pretty obvious that Oldman didn't trust George Finley much," Jerry said.

"I have to agree with Oldman's opinion there. I thought he was a snake," I said. "Well, we are still left with two unsolved murders—and a missing daughter. And legal papers missing from a locked filing cabinet."

He looked at me. "You don't suppose that George Finley removed them himself and hid them somewhere?"

"He would have relocked the cabinet to protect the files that were left in the drawer, if he was the one who removed them." We were both quiet, thinking, then I said, "You might think about getting a court order and seeing if George had a safe deposit box, and take a look inside, for one thing, just to be sure." I thought, but didn't say out loud: *Not that we'll be that lucky.*

"How about if I petition the court for you to be George Finley's executor—or administrator?"

"I'm sure he has a will naming an executor—and anyway, don't even *joke* about a thing like that, even if you are a cop. Or I'll slap you silly," I said, smirking, my sense of humor returning a bit.

He laughed, and I was surprised he took that remark so well. A lot of cops wouldn't take a remark like that, on general principles. And I'd get the you-know-what beat out of me. "I appreciate the pickle you're in—we're both in," he said. "I'm sorry about you being Reilly's executor if you don't want to be. Sounds like an awful lot of work. I never realized that. And I'm not happy that murders have happened here in town. But Faith Christine likes you, and I do, too."

He finished his coffee. I sat, still angry. Feeling guilty for being angry at a dead man for making me executor without asking or telling me. I'd known of estates that take years and years to settle. I hoped that this wouldn't be one of them.

It sounded like in this case, the biggest creditor might be the federal government, if in messing around with Jessica's estate, George Finley had neglected to pay taxes properly.

If it fell to Oldman's estate. Maybe it didn't. It sounded

like it maybe it didn't, according to Jerry. It depended on how complex both wills were.

And if there was anything left.

I had the right to refuse to be executor. But what did I owe Oldman? What did I owe his children?

An executor has the obligation to do the job with loyalty and care and a minimum loss of cash to beneficiaries.

"Any sign of that crazy guy with the scar on his chin from the mining thing?"

"No," Jerry said. "You warn Faith Christine?"

"Yes," I said. "I called her."

Jerry said, "Well, I've gotta go." He stood up, put his cup neatly in the sink, and left.

I needed to talk to Faith Christine about all that had happened, and I'd already promised to spend the night there.

I grabbed a clean shirt, jeans, socks, shaving things, and other things I needed and jammed them in a paper bag from the grocery store. I stuck the lawyer's fancy maroon folder in the bag and put them on the couch.

Maybe at Faith Christine's, I could study them further.

I cleaned up, took my stuff, locked up, and drove to Faith Christine's. As far as I could figure, Faith Christine was safe now, and so was I. If it was the mining company, they'd have had no reason to kill Finley. He had nothing to do with that. The killings had been messy and up-close. Rage. If the mining company had sent someone to kill Oldman, it would be bullets, not the bloody way he had been killed. Unless it was that crazy Thomas Smith guy with the scar on his chin. But Faith Christine and I would have been his targets, not the lawyer, who had done nothing but write a letter. I tended toward the Oldman family and Jessica's money, maybe, being the focus now for the murders, not the mining fracas.

Chapter Twelve

It was too late for Peter. Ken was all googly-eyed over Arlene, who had come over to stay with and protect Patricia. And Arlene was all googly-eyed back at Ken.

It was nice to see that the sisters stuck together, but it was more like a party than a "protection" atmosphere in the living room.

Faith Christine steered me gently into the kitchen from her living room, where the four of them had gathered, eating cake and cookies and drinking coffee and sodas. We stood next to her pine trestle kitchen table in front of the big picture window.

Fiercely she whispered, "What's with you and Pat Jacobsen?"

I didn't know what the heck she was talking about. I put my paper bag full of stuff down on the table. I had left the Finley legal papers locked in the truck for the time being.

"She's been driving us all crazy with 'John is wonderful . . . John did this . . . John said that,' " Faith Christine said in a low voice. "She thinks you rescued her."

"I am flattered," I began, like a fool.

"Flattered," Faith Christine said. "Flattered!" I knew I had said the wrong thing when her eyes narrowed.

"Well, I—"

"You better 'Well, I—' " she said.

"I was thinking that she and Peter . . ."

"Oh," Faith Christine said, and she unpuffed like a hen smoothing down her feathers after the danger is past.

I said, "Though I thought maybe he would like Arlene . . ."

"Ken has already claimed Arlene," she said.

"I saw."

"Well, you don't have to worry."

"Why? And about what?" I said. "I could use a break from worrying," I said sarcastically.

"Oh," she said. "Sorry. I forgot you have been through a lot lately. I just meant about Pat, in there, being after you."

"She's not *after* me," I said. "For Pete's sake, she's my son's age."

"You didn't hear her bragging about you. Even went so far as to say you're handsome. And, well, as I said, you don't have to worry. I told her that you were . . . mine, so to speak," Faith Christine said.

I smiled, and I reached for her and pulled her close to me, which wasn't far because she was already standing very close as we whispered.

"C'mon, what are you thinking of, Faith Christine? You were just recently complaining that I . . ."

"That was before," she said, nuzzling a place deep on the side of my neck which gave me goosebumps down both arms. "This is now," she finished.

We both heard Peter's voice in the living room. My heart was glad to hear that wonderful deep voice. Faith Christine and I broke apart and went in the living room to greet him.

"I know where to find my dad, if he's not at home," he said jokingly to Faith Christine, after giving her a hug.

I looked, and Patricia was sitting up straighter in her chair; I was hopeful that that might indicate some interest.

In a few minutes, Peter and I were left alone in the kitchen. I was proud of how clean-cut and handsome he was. He looked so much like Dora around his eyes, and his chin.

We sat at the table, Faith Christine having supplied my son with coffee, and he whispered, "What's going on?"

He leaned intently toward me over the table.

"There's been two murders . . . and now you're going to be executor—which, Lord knows—and so does everybody this side of the Mississippi—that you *hate* being? And of Oldman's estate? Isn't he almost a pauper? Not that anybody calls it that now . . . wasn't he, like a recluse? More than even you?"

"What do you mean, 'more than even me?' I'm not a recluse."

"You wouldn't leave here and come and live in Los Angeles near me, like I wanted you to, after Mom died."

He looked around at Faith Christine's nice kitchen, and said, "Of course, I can understand that now, to a certain extent."

"I'm not a recluse. I do like my privacy, though," I conceded. "I like my life, for the most part."

He knew I was talking about losing his mother.

He shut up. Then he tried again. "I brought—" He looked toward the living room, and then looked back at me as if to decide what to say next, in case anyone was listening. "—what you wanted. At least what I could find. I left it out in my car."

He looked at me. "Do you want me to bring it inside, or wait till we get home?"

"Bring it inside. I assume you are spending the night at our house?"

"I plan on staying at home, if you want me, until the funeral."

I knew without his directly saying so, that he was worried and had come to help. I felt a rush of love for him. And pride. "Thank you," I said. "I want you to very much."

He left.

Faith Christine came in the kitchen, and chuckled, if you could call a woman's laugh like that a chuckle, and said, "Make up another bed?"

"I believe so," I said.

She left to follow Peter out to his car to tell him to bring his suitcase in and spend the night here.

I had a lot to talk about with Peter, since he had left for here and never got my last set of messages.

He remembered Arlene, and had said so during the introductions, but there was an awful lot to fill him in on.

It was getting so I couldn't keep track of what I had told to whom. Jerry, Faith Christine, and now Peter, as well as everyone else I had talked to.

The biggest wild card was Beth.

Had Peter found out anything?

I couldn't wait to find out, and I needed to talk to him

alone. He brought in his suitcase, and he handed me a pile of papers. I took them out and locked them in my truck with the other papers, since there was no lock on Faith Christine's bedroom doors.

I wanted to fill Peter in first. The information might be easier to digest when there were two people thinking about it.

Patricia and Faith Christine were inside cooking supper, and Ken and Arlene were still sitting in the living room, engrossed in each other.

Peter and I walked out to take a look at the mules, corralled near the barn. We watched them in silence. I was glad just to be in Peter's company.

There was only the light that Christine had up high, attached to near the top of the barn, shining down on the corral. It was a pleasant scene. Peaceful on the surface.

"I really like it here," Peter said. "I miss the beauty and quiet." I had to agree; it was one reason Dora and I had moved here from New York City.

All of a sudden one of the mules reared up enough to come down hard on its front feet, and began stamping. Peter and I hurried over, although I knew what it was.

"Mules are smart," I said to Peter, admiringly. Sure enough, one of the six mules had just killed—crushed to death—a western diamondback rattler which had had the bad fortune to crawl inside the corral, probably heading toward the barn in search of rodents to eat. A night hunter.

We walked over, close, to see. I'm one of those people who think that a rattler is an awe-inspiring creature.

We bent over to examine the flattened snake, but not too close. Five rattles. Not an old-timer. Thin, like it hadn't eaten in a while.

The murderer we sought was like a human rattler close by—or someone more dangerous—the kind of creature that *didn't* do you the courtesy of rattling a warning before striking.

This particular rattler was dead, however, and showed one of the reasons why in the Gold Rush days, the prospectors had loved their mules: mules hate rattlers, and they'll kill them when they can.

I went to Faith Christine's unlocked equipment shed and got a rake. As I removed the dead rattler out of the corral with the rake, I told Peter every single thing I knew about what was going on, starting at the beginning as I dragged the body of the limp snake a good distance away. Then I leaned the rake up against the wall of the barn and went back to stand beside Peter. We stood close together with our arms folded over the rail of the corral, watching the mules as we talked.

I told him that earlier, I had intended to go on a physical search for Beth by driving and visiting each psychiatric facility near here, going to the closest first, and moving on out in a widening circle, but that so far, I hadn't had a chance.

I told him I was hoping that what he had brought me—his computer research, which I'd just locked in my truck—could save me the trouble. I told him that Jerry hadn't had any luck locating her, either. So far.

"Two years ago she disappeared after leaving Tranquility House, and she had some kind of falling out with her brother Charles about that time," I told him. "I intend to go through all Oldman's papers as soon as I get the go-ahead from Jerry . . . after the funeral is soon enough, legally."

We went in and ate, and much later, we found ourselves back out at the corrals again. We leaned over the top poles and talked further.

"Faith Christine is arranging that all bills for the funeral be sent to me," I told him, "and she's called the newspaper about his obituary. They covered his murder; it made the front page, of course."

"It's hard to believe that all this was going on—Mr. Reilly and all his troubles with his children—and we hardly knew about it," Peter said. "I knew Chuck in school, but we hung around in different groups—we weren't even close. In fact, I hardly knew him."

I guessed he was suggesting that "Chuck" was hanging around with the small local group that did drugs.

"What did you find out about Beth?"

"I brought computer printouts of all that I found. Very little—actually nothing—about the last two years, so it might not be much help. She seems to have disappeared. She could have died out of state," he said. "But I think that that would show up somewhere. No current or past California motor vehicle licenses under Beth Reilly. No psychiatric commitments in the last two years. No marriage."

"Any clues as to what was wrong with her?"

"No."

He looked at me. "I think that George Finley knew where she is . . . because, from what you've said, he acted so secretive."

"Or, he didn't want me to know, for some reason, that *he* had lost track of her. He wanted me to *think* he knew."

"That could be," Peter admitted.

I looked at my watch. It was past two in the morning,

again, but I was wide awake. The mules were quiet, but they were still attentive and alert.

"These are smart mules," Peter admitted.

"I have a fondness for them as well," I said.

"If I ever move out of L.A., I wouldn't mind having a few mules," Peter said unexpectedly.

"I thought you loved L.A.," I said.

He ignored that.

"How do you like Patricia?" I asked.

"She's pretty, real pretty," he admitted.

I decided to leave well enough alone. For now. I went inside. Jerry called. "Sorry I'm calling so late. But the mining guy's brother—you know, Thomas Smith with the scar on his chin. He's been located. He ran away with his best friend's wife. To Las Vegas. It's a romance thing, not a revenge thing, that caused his disappearance."

"Thanks for calling, Jerry. It's always good to have one less thing to worry about."

I hung up.

Chapter Thirteen

Faith Christine and I were the only two people still up. Everyone else had just gone to bed and their doors were closed. I sat in the living room on the couch next to Faith Christine. I wanted to talk to her a minute, even though I was tired. It was three o'clock in the morning. It was hard to believe all that had happened since our fight Sunday afternoon.

"I think your son is thinking about moving back here," Faith Christine said.

I was irked. "How did you find that out?" I said, trusting that because she said it, it was the truth, and hurt because my son had told her first instead of telling me.

"He did try to feel you out he said, but you didn't seem too enthused," she said.

"What?" I said. "Of course I'd be enthused. I'd love it if Peter moved closer. I hate driving all the way down to

L.A. to see him. It would be great. Why didn't he just say so?"

"Men!" Faith Christine said softly. "He said he did try to tell you when you were out pulling the snake out of the corral."

"Oh." Somehow I didn't pick up on it just that way. "I guess the snake kind of threw me off," I said. "He was just saying something about liking it here when the mule went after the snake."

"He says he was trying to tell you that he wanted to move back home."

"Back *home?*"

"Just until he finds his own place, of course."

I groaned.

"It wouldn't be until next month, or even longer. He has to give notice at his apartment."

"What about his job?"

"You really ought to talk to him about all this—but his office is what they call 'decentralizing,' and that means that he can work out of his home. He gets the work sent to him over the phone lines, and then he just does it on his computer and sends it back out or faxes it or something. It's supposed to save the cost of running a big office."

"Decentralizing?"

"Yup."

"Hmm."

"He says he has enough money to buy a place up here."

"Probably does." He did mention buying mules.

"He might be able to help you . . . you know, solve everything."

"Probably will."

"You should sound a little happier," Faith Christine said.

"I had a few plans myself," I said, picturing myself and the pretty lady next to me.

"I hope they include me," she said.

"They all did . . . and do," I said, giving her a nuzzle on her neck.

"Stop that," she said, not moving a muscle, in fact opening her neck up even more.

"All right," I said, moving around to give her what I hoped was a decent kiss.

A few minutes later I went out to my truck while Faith Christine was fussing around getting ready to go to sleep. I couldn't believe we were up so late.

I had reached my truck, unlocked the door, and was reaching underneath the seat to where I had hidden all the papers, when I thought I heard a noise.

I froze, and listened. I thought I heard it again.

Should I call out "Who's there?" Just moving my eyes, not my body, I looked as far around as I could. I doubted that anyone was in the barn, or the mules would be letting me know—especially if it was a stranger.

There it was again, the noise of quiet footsteps behind me. My heart started pounding. "Ken! You scared the life out of me," I said. "I thought you were in bed." Ken looked upset. "Mr. Ranger, it was you who said to be careful, and to watch out. I'm a police officer, and I'm just doing my job. Besides, I thought that *you* must have gone to bed by now. Then I saw you out here, and—"

I relaxed. What was I thinking of? I was thinking of him as one of the group and not as a police officer guarding us. Of course he hadn't just gone to bed.

"—I thought we'd discuss shifts—guard duty, so to speak," he said, in a voice that sounded apologetic.

"My apologies to you, Ken. I think I'm overtired."

"Peter said he will take four in the morning until eight," Ken said.

"Then how about if I take from now till then," I said. I had to stay up anyway to study Peter's printouts and re-study Finley's stuff. "You can take from eight A.M. on, Ken."

"I thought you said you were tired," he said.

"I'm wide awake now," I said jokingly. But it was the truth. He had scared me wide awake. "And it's only one more hour," I said, looking at my watch.

"I'll tell Peter when I wake him up, that it's your turn after his," I promised.

"Okay," he said, as he retreated toward the house.

I guess my nerves were more shot than I realized.

I decided not to turn off the overhead light by the barn, as I had been planning, and to leave it on all night.

I got the folder Finley had given me and Peter's computer printouts from under the seat of the truck, locked my truck, and went back inside. In the kitchen, I put the papers on the table. I sat at the pine trestle table near the picture window. Someone had covered up the window again with the blanket as a precaution.

Perhaps we were being foolish worrying about a rifle shot from a distance, but nothing about this mess would surprise me anymore, even though so far the killer or killers had been knife-wielding instead of gun-toting.

I read everything through once. Then I checked through them again, studying them intently.

Finally, discouraged, I spread a few of the pages from Finley's office out on the table, and in the quiet, something Oldman said occurred to me.

If I remembered right, he said something like, "I used to know enough to pull off the trail once in a while to see if the bad guys were behind me."

He didn't consider himself one of the bad guys.

What did that mean, if anything?

He'd just had an experience where someone was trying to trick him to get access to his property. Yet, even though he'd be extra cautious because of that, he'd let someone get close enough to kill him. Who? And why?

I sorted though Finley's paperwork again. There was a copy of the sternly worded letter George had sent to the mining company threatening to sue for fraud and misrepresentation for the five thousand they had offered Oldman Reilly for use of his land as access.

It was written well enough, I'd have to give Finley that. Threatening well was evidently one of his skills.

Things were beginning to become a little clearer as I did some calculating, using dates scattered throughout the paperwork.

By my calculations, Jessica must have been a lot younger than her husband Oldman. Why didn't I think of that before?

I only knew Oldman the last twenty years. From when he was sixty-five to eighty-five. His oldest daughter was thirty. Eighty-five minus thirty was fifty-five. Old to be becoming a father, particularly in those days.

Any date of their marriage in this mess of papers? I sorted through. Yes. Jessica Shaw was thirty-four. May-

December marriage, then. Things were even clearer. Fifty-three-year-old man, thirty-four-year-old woman.

Funny a rich heiress marrying so late—but she was supposed to be sickly all her life. I still didn't know what the cause or the illness was. No one else seemed to know either.

The first adoption was two years later, when Jessica was thirty-six, and Oldman was fifty-five, which I had already calculated.

Charles was adopted two years later; he was now twenty-eight. Jessica died a year after his adoption.

Whew. If you're that ill, is it fair to the children? Well, it explained why normal adoption procedures were probably out of the question. And Oldman might have been too old to qualify for a regular adoption through proper channels. I tended to lean toward the theory that Oldman was probably an unwilling participant in the bogus adoption thing. That would explain his attitude toward the children as well as his lack of papers—at least, Jerry hadn't mentioned any—at his house involving the adoptions.

Plus his feeling that he was not one of the bad guys.

No wonder Charles was screwed up; not that I condoned drug-taking as a problem-solving device, ever.

Where was Beth? Did she do it? Did she blame Oldman and Finley for her troubles? Or was she an innocent victim? Faith Christine didn't like Beth. And she likes just about *everybody.* Is that a bad sign?

In fact, she didn't want to come with me on my search for Beth. A search that I'd better begin tomorrow. I had to face the fact that I'd been putting it off. I expected to talk to some depressing matron somewhere who would tell me that Beth was a tragic case who cut her own arms to make herself bleed, or something. A self-mutilator, or something gruesome like that.

Chapter Fourteen

"**N**o, not self-destructive, or anything like that," Mrs. Eunice Wilson said haughtily, as we sat in her bare-looking, yellow-painted, cement-walled office talking in Harmony Hall. I got the name of the place from Peter's computer list. The big round white clock with black plastic trim in back of her, over her head, said 11:31.

"Heard voices. God talking to her, stuff like that. Burned crosses on things every chance she got . . . purifying things that had been touched by 'sinners.' "

Great. Schizophrenic, although Eunice Wilson was careful not to actually say so. She made it clear that she wasn't telling anything confidential—just giving me "general information."

Harmony Hall was one of those places—which all look similar to me—used by families frightened of a family member's behavior. It was an hour-and-a-half drive from Rushing River Junction.

Built in the fifties, it was supposed to look like a campus,

111

one-story cinderblock buildings laid out so that one room didn't look into another, but into a courtyard. Cement everywhere; wire grids over the windows. Inside, lots of pale yellow walls, supposed to make you cheerful.

Beth had been in and out of there various times between the ages of eight and seventeen. When she was eighteen she had had to leave. Eighteen was the upper age limit to stay at Harmony House.

She'd been transferred on the day of her eighteenth birthday to Heal the Breach House.

Her last day sounded brutal, the way Mrs. Wilson described it. A birthday party during "snack time" in the morning, and in the afternoon a transfer to a new place.

Mrs. Wilson didn't seem aware of the harshness of doing that. Like throwing someone out of the house.

I wondered how Beth felt about that.

Eunice Wilson was aware of Oldman Reilly's death; she had seen it in the newspapers and been "extremely shocked" as she called it, and that was why she was doing all she could to help out—within the boundaries of confidentiality.

No, she didn't have any photos, but Beth was tending toward heaviness due to the side effects of the strong medication, had straight hair, and blue-gray eyes. Five-foot-two. I told her that her "general information," as she called it, about Beth had been very helpful. It was; it was the first concrete information on Beth that I had been able to obtain. From anybody.

I left, after I realized that that was all I was going to get out of her. Mrs. Wilson seemed like a tough woman, but fair. She was a "rules are rules" kind of person. I guess there's nothing wrong with that. Usually.

I called home from the nearest gas station to talk to Peter and Faith Christine, but nobody answered, so I was off to Heal the Breach House, eighteen miles south down the road toward San Francisco.

Heal the Breach House was larger and more impersonal than Harmony House. Strictly for adults.

The lady in charge was less helpful than Mrs. Wilson, to say the least. I drove up and parked, and was just getting out of my truck, when a woman rushed out of the building and came across the parking lot, over to me. She never introduced herself, or did anything but act as if I were a dirty fly that had flown in and must be removed as soon as possible. The brush-off, or perhaps the squash-off.

Didn't even wait for me to get out of my truck and come to the door. Blow-dried dyed blond hair, fancy black dress, nylons, black heels, lots of real gold circle bracelets jangling on her wrists over her Rolex watch. Tiny figure, big overbearing nose. A warning light went on in my head from her attitude.

"I'm sorry," she said, like she wasn't. "We don't allow any guests, or anybody coming for a visit that wasn't pre-planned." Haughty and extremely annoyed. I obviously wasn't going to be allowed inside.

Her excuse was that she was too busy today to talk with me; perhaps if I had made an appointment—

Too busy? There were only five or six cars in the parking lot. They looked like a bunch of very underpaid employees' cars. One late-model luxury Cadillac with customized gold trim, probably hers. I left, trying to give her the impression, without really saying so, that I would not be back.

I decided that "perhaps" my next visit would also be a surprise visit, with Jerry and maybe Ken along as witnesses. "Perhaps" we'd see how she liked that. The hairs stand up on the back of my neck when places like that don't like or allow visitors—especially unannounced. That usually means that they have to have time to hide what it is they are doing that they shouldn't be. If you've nothing to hide, and you're proud of what you are doing, you're open to visits and visitors in reasonable amounts and conditions. This was not a state-run place, but an expensive private facility.

The place gave me the shivers.

Happy eighteenth birthday, Beth.

To give Jerry Vivens due credit, we were back knocking on the door of Heal the Breach House in less than five hours, giving the witch not that much time to cover her rear. He had with him every State Inspector he could scare up on short notice.

I had called Jerry from the nearest pay phone and he drove right over, once I had explained what was going on. Might have been speeding, he got there so quick.

I waited for him just down the road, out of sight of the place, at the nearest gas station.

He walked into Heal the Breach House unannounced, holding his badge up in plain sight. I was following behind him. She gave me a very dirty look.

I smiled.

Surprise, surprise. The conditions inside were deplorable, and the woman's attitude made a quick-change from haughty to beggingly groveling to Jerry. She didn't want Jerry to report the conditions inside. It wasn't going to work. Jerry was beyond angry. On-the-verge-of-punching-someone angry. The patients were underwashed, underfed, overmedicated, and painfully skinny, which said a lot about what they were getting—or not getting—to eat, considering the side effects of some of the medicines for mental illnesses include weight gain. Or even not considering it.

And the bed sores.

She decided to be helpful as a part of the groveling toward Jerry, trying (I knew fruitlessly) to gain his goodwill.

Beth had run away four or five times. Finally the family had removed her, but not until two years had passed.

Visitors were discouraged, the woman said, so that patients would "adjust better." She felt it was too emotionally draining on the patients to have loved ones come and then leave, leaving the patients behind. They were upset for days after each visit, the woman said.

Of course, I thought. Your family visited you and you hadn't been rescued. How betrayed by their family can a human being feel?

And translate that to unannounced visitors were not welcome so that they wouldn't catch on to what was going on.

Beth had never adjusted, she said. *Good for you, Beth,* I mentally cheered her.

They did have, once a month, "Family Day," she said. Once a month she dressed them and cleaned them up, she meant. Probably fed them decently for a week or so before.

The employees crept around meekly, I could see, terrified of Mrs. Frick. Sometimes, employees are the ones who "rat out" a place like this to the authorities; these poor people looked as beaten down and as frightened as the patients. But they got to go home at night. They should have told. I was angry at them as well, but not as much as I was at Mrs. Frick, Cadillac owner.

Jerry asked Mrs. Frick if he could use her phone. He was deliberately trying to annoy her, as he had his cell phone.

To my surprise, he called a friend of his—Faith Christine's brother, the State Supreme Court judge.

The woman was staring daggers at us, trying to intimidate us, no longer pretending to be nice, and we sat there, like two war parties, for the half hour it took for a bunch of cops to arrive and start taking photos, getting everything on tape, and ramming Mrs. Frick to the wall—figuratively speaking, of course.

Evidently when this State Supreme Court judge spoke, the earth rumbled around him in all directions.

It didn't make me feel any better, though; it instead made me feel sick and sad, as it always did, that humans treat one another so badly to make a buck. Or many bucks. People who make their living victimizing those who are least able to defend themselves. Makes me sick; makes Jerry *mad.* Mad as hell. Finally, we were able to leave. I made a statement on tape about how when I arrived she wouldn't let me in, and I got suspicious about bad conditions.

I'd be going to court in about two years, I guessed, to testify, the way these things dragged out.

Jerry said, "I'm going to close that place down immediately, if it's the last thing I do. Did you see the filth in the kitchen? Did you see the huge pile of—"

I nodded. The patients had been tied down. Although she had gotten the leather straps off them just in time, evidently, many still had indentation marks on their bodies, some like the marks that your eyeglasses leave on your nose when you have worn them for years. Showed up good on the tape, the taping guy said.

Jerry went to his car, still sputtering. The proper authorities would be taking over from here.

Usually, they're pretty good. I don't know how this particular place had gotten away with it so long.

They may have gradually deteriorated.

But Beth had run away.

I knew myself well enough to know I would feel bad about that place for days. I got in my truck and drove off. I needed to go home.

At home, there were messages from both daughters wondering why I hadn't called recently. Claire, calling from New York City, insinuated that she knew I was "busy" with Faith Christine. She said it in a joking way. How do women know these things when I barely had found out myself?

Ann had seen in the newspapers about Oldman. She lived in San Jose. The newspapers there were tying the death to the mining troubles, she said in the message, and she asked "Are you and Faith Christine in any danger?" Her message finished: "Call me back as soon as you get this message."

Both daughters were married, with children. I was glad that they were far enough away to be out of this mess.

I called them both back, and they both were out. I left them fairly long messages explaining what was going on and reassuring them that I didn't think it was the mining corporation behind it, so Faith Christine and I were not in danger. I included messages to my grandchildren, saying, "I love you."

I'd have to remember to put a couple of bucks in some envelopes to send to the grandchildren, like I usually did.

I needed to eat, and sit a minute.

I needed to give Faith Christine some money later; she'd been feeding an army over there, and it wasn't fair for her to have to do that. I got three hundred dollars out of my cash stash in the bottom of my sock drawer, and tucked it in one of my trouser pockets to give to her later.

I needed to go through the growing pile of mail that was mounding up—about four inches high of mail—mostly junk mail, but I knew that there were rental checks from properties I owned in Los Angeles in the pile.

When I moved out west with Dora, we had liquidated our real estate in New York, and it bought a lot more property at that time, with California prices compared to New York City prices then. We purchased two low-end rental properties—about twenty-nine thousand each, at the time.

We fixed them up and rented them out. We figured low-end rentals would never be vacant, and we were right. We didn't count on the boom in Los Angeles prices. The craziness as prices went up.

A hotel chain wanted to purchase one of the homes to rip down to build a new hotel. We ended up leasing the land to them and got a hefty check each year.

The other little house increased in value to about a hundred and twenty-nine thousand. Rental profits increased as the neighborhood went upscale: people fixed up the little thirties-style houses to raise families in.

With the profits, Dora and I had bought more properties over the years and fixed them up. Which was a blessing, as the ranch was not a huge moneymaker.

The rentals provided about half of my income, these days.

My Gray Mist ranch property hadn't cost much twenty years ago—and although worth more now, it was not financial considerations that kept me here; far from it.

It would be easier, as Peter had often reminded me, to manage my properties if I relocated nearer to Los Angeles.

Over the years, I had assembled a list of reputable repairmen who took care of anything that went wrong with the rentals.

It was the beauty here, and the people. Most of the people here were good people. Good-hearted people. With a few notable exceptions, who I seemed to be running into a lot lately, with all this business.

I dumped a can of chili into a small saucepan and put it on the stove to heat, and decided to take a quick look through one of the newspapers which had piled up, unread.

I went into the living room, picked up one of the newspapers, sat on the couch, and read. I jumped up, smelling something coming from in the kitchen. I hurried in there; the chili had popped and sputtered all over the stove, and made a mess. I grabbed a dishrag, wet it, and mopped off the stove. Then I plopped the chili in a bowl, grabbed some saltine crackers to crush in it so it would be more filling, got some ice water out of the refrigerator, and took a spoon out of the silverware drawer.

I took it all with me into the back bedroom on the left which served as my office.

Sitting at my desk, taking occasional mouthfuls of the chili, I began to sort through the stack of mail, sorting it into two basic piles. One was junk mail and what I call "begging letters"—letters from every charity humans ever thought of. I seem to be a favorite on hundreds of lists. I'd cope with that pile later. It was huge.

The other pile was important, real mail. Piles of bills, and rental payments. Cards, letters, and once in a while special payment from a fellow New York lawyer—now a millionaire—who kept me on retainer for research work.

When he was considering a merger or an acquisition, he

would call me and I'd research the background of that company or corporation for him. Sometimes I physically went and looked around the place for him, sized it up, and wrote a report.

It was work that I enjoyed doing, and brought me an occasional change of pace from shoveling manure from the livestock, and caring for my fruit trees and garden.

I left the two stacks on my desk, ready to work on, as I scooped out the last drippy bite of the chili.

I got up, went outside, and looked up at the stars for a few minutes. My usual schedule had been all messed up since the whole Oldman thing. I'd been up real late two nights in a row. I'd be glad when this was over, and things could get back, or close, to normal; realistically, I knew something had changed forever with Oldman's death.

I went back inside, and called my daughters again. They were fine, and both worried about me. I reassured them.

Then I tackled the two piles. I reconciled my checkbook, paid current bills and I almost decided against even bothering with the pile of "begging" letters.

There were a few charities that I liked to give to, however, and after sticking a few dollars in envelopes to each of my grandchildren, I tackled the pile.

Some went directly in the garbage, and I almost heaved one from Our Lady of Perpetual Humility—stupid name, I thought—when I saw that it had a Los Angeles address. An address near the Barrio. But it had a Priority Mail sticker on it.

I ripped the envelope open. Inside was a letter from— my guess was that it was a storefront—Sister Esmeralda Juantez. There was no date. The writing was even but fairly large and leaned heavily back to the left.

My dear Mr. Ranger:

It has come to my attention that you are attempting to locate Beth Reilly. A man named Peter called and said you were hunting for a Beth Reilly. I was not here at the time. The people here that day were new, and not aware of Beth. She comes and goes, and the last time I saw her here at the mission was two months ago. When she comes again, I will do my best to get her to contact you. She will be calling you collect, probably, as she has no money, and our mission is poor, also. She is presently homeless. She is a poor, lost lamb of God. We do what we can for her. I have gotten your number from Information, and will provide it to her when she comes. I hope this is helpful.

Sincerely yours, in service to Christ,
Sister Esmeralda

Under her name, in pencil, was a hand-drawn cross, very tiny. Almost microscopic.

I had almost thrown the letter away. One of my faults—judging by appearances. The letter looked like a begging letter judging by the envelope.

Darn it! My conscience would make me open and check every begging letter I got for a long time now.

I quickly scribbled out a note of thanks and inserted a check for fifty bucks in an envelope. I said in the note that a collect call would be fine, and I wanted to help Beth as best I could. I signed it, sealed the envelope, and put it with the rest, ready to mail.

Peter's research had done some good, after all.

I hoped that Finley hadn't stolen all the money. I had a feeling that Beth might do well in a small group home, maybe five or six patients and a house staff. Close, caring people to see that medications were taken on time. A "family" group situation. I just hoped that there was enough left in Jessica's trust fund to do something like that.

If Beth wasn't a murderer.

I had eliminated Charles, pretty much. Was I wrong?

Did I owe either one of them the truth about their adoptions? Or did Beth already know?

Did either one of them know or suspect?

I am rotten about talking about intimate things with young people. What do you do? Just bring it up? How? Do you pussyfoot first and try to see what they know? A person with my size boots doesn't know how to pussyfoot too well. And being six-foot-three doesn't aid me in pussyfooting ability, either. Not to mention being "reticent", as I have been (falsely) accused of being by you-know-who.

But I thought I had a solution.

Faith Christine.

Chapter Fifteen

"I want you to ask Charles about Beth, and about Old-man. Pump him for all you can find out," I said. "Like, does he know he is adopted? Does he know Beth is? Does she know? What was their fight two years ago about—"

"Whoa, pardner, slow down there," Faith Christine said, as she let me into her house that evening.

I had dropped my completed bill envelopes, the letter to Our Lady of Perpetual Humility, and the grandchildren letters in the blue mailbox in front of the tiny post office building in Rushing River Junction before I came.

"A while ago I called you John Wayne. Now you've turned into Sherlock Holmes," she said, joking, as we walked through the living room into her kitchen. A big peach pie was on the counter, one piece already missing.

"No, more like Clouseau in *The Pink Panther*," I said.

"Or Bugs Bunny. I'm beginning to think I have multiple personality disorder," I joked.

She smiled. "Pie?"

"Perfect," I answered.

"Vanilla ice cream on top?"

"Even more perfect."

She cut me a big piece, added the ice cream on top, and set it in front of me. I took a bite. Umm. Smelled good and just a little bit warm yet. Ice cream melting just the tiniest bit into the peach chunks and goo. I took another bite.

"I'm surprised the phone isn't ringing," I said. "Every time I'm enjoying a minute's peace, something happens lately, Watson."

"What are you going to do next?"

"I'm not sure. Right after the funeral, I want to check with Tranquility House—that's the place Beth was supposedly at last. She was there up until two years ago. Then she disappeared. I wish I had access to a copy of Jessica's will. That might explain things. I want to find out *why* the Shaw file was stolen, if I can."

"Do you think the killer is—was—related to either Oldman or Jessica? Or could it be that someone didn't want the fact to come out that the kids were adopted, or that the adoption was illegal? Maybe someone local who helped with the adoptions that we don't know about?"

"We won't know the answers to that until I do a lot of checking. I'd like to know what is in George Finley's safe deposit box, too," I said. "How are the funeral arrangements coming along?"

"Fine. We're keeping it very simple, under the circumstances."

I nodded approval. "Good."

"We'd like you to say a few words," she added.

"Great," I said, trying to keep the sarcasm in my voice to a bare minimum.

"Tomorrow morning, at nine-thirty at the First Baptist," she said.

"I'll be there," I said.

"Charles is going to stay here, with Miss Whitaker," she said. "They're arriving tonight, late."

"You're going to be crowded. Peter and I will stay at my house tonight."

"You don't need to do that," she said regretfully.

"I have a lot to do," I said truthfully.

"Jerry is pulling Ken off duty here tomorrow morning," she said. "He thinks the murders had nothing to do with the mining claims."

"No, I guess not" I said. "Certainly George Finley had very little to do with the mining claim thing, other than writing that one threatening letter. I tend to agree with Jerry, but I wish you'd still be careful until we find out who killed George and Oldman."

"I will," she said. "But I liked having you sleep over here and protect us," she said, smiling at me with that friendly, warm expression that I liked so much.

"I wasn't much protection" I said.

"You helped Ken by telling him what to do," she said.

"Is Patricia Jacobsen going to be staying here, going home, or going to stay with her aunt?" I asked. With Ken gone, maybe the Great Dane would be useful.

"I'm not sure. We haven't talked it over yet. But Jerry thinks it might be safe for her to go home. It appears that it was just George Finley that the murderer was after. Pat mentioned going to stay with her aunt tomorrow night."

She smiled again. "Maybe Peter better go and make friends with the Great Dane if she decides to go and stay with her aunt," she said.

"You think Peter is interested in Pat?" I asked.

She nodded yes.

"Seems to be coming along fine," she said.

Peter and Pat. I liked the sound of that. I said so. Faith Christine laughed.

We weren't laughing the next morning at Oldman's funeral. The cops were there, of course, to see who came. Hardly anybody. Lived that many years and hardly a soul thought it worth attending his funeral. Sad.

Beth hadn't shown up, something which I had to admit secretly I was counting on. I thought somehow she would have gotten the news—it was on TV—and made it here.

Charles was there with Miss Whitaker. He looked sad, but my guess was that it was sadness more for himself than for Oldman. And I guess, also, that he had the right to feel that way.

Faith Christine met me outside the small white Baptist church on the other side of town from our homes, and we walked inside together. We sat near the front of the church. Peter was in the row in front of us with Patricia and Arlene. Jerry was standing at the back with Ken.

Other police officers were in plainclothes in the church. I recognized most of the people there. Esther Cooper, the egg lady who had found the body, was there. Faith Christine's three sons wouldn't be able to make it. Henry, Junior, was in the Air Force and stationed at Pensacola, Florida. Albert was a horse trainer in Wyoming, and Paul was in Paris, studying French for a year. Faith Christine was all dressed up in a black suit. She looked very nice. She whispered to me that she hadn't had a chance to talk to Charles at all, since he and Miss Whitaker arrived very late and went right to sleep. And this morning, she whispered, she didn't feel right asking questions when his father was about to be buried.

"I'll take care of it, later," I whispered back.

I said my few words. Nobody else spoke except for the minister. I told the truth about Oldman as I saw it. He was a man who appeared to try to do the right thing, as he saw it. That was the basic theme of my talk. I said he and his father were both carpenters, and how he had valued his father's saw. I said how he had wanted to save the mountain. Without lying, I said what I could honestly say. It didn't take long.

There were a few scattered mourners, some people from the three Rushing River Junction churches who feel obligated to attend any funeral where they feel that a community member will otherwise go unmourned.

I had to admire them just a bit, grudgingly. They were probably better human beings than I am. People who attended Bible-study groups, and for whom the Church is their family. Mostly older people, but a few women in their thirties.

Nobody weird, unexpected, criminal-looking, or bizarre attended the short service at the Baptist church or at the graveside. Nobody out of place. No complete strangers. I did see some of the church ladies looking askance at Charles's shaved head and eyebrow piercings.

Nobody talked much; it was one of the most silent funerals I've ever attended. Nobody cried, although everyone was quiet and respectful.

What an ending. A life which had appeared to be usual and normal on the surface but had had such hidden secrets and surprises. Are all lives like that? I didn't think so. Mine wasn't. And I didn't know the half of it yet, about Oldman's private life, not having gone through his papers. I suspected that there was also a lot more to be found in George Finley's stolen files, if they were ever found or recovered. What a mess.

We left the grave site. We were all going back to Faith Christine's, where she had prepared food for everyone. I had given her the three hundred dollars the night before when we talked. I let her assume it was from Oldman's estate.

Charles was going to ride in my truck with me, and Miss Whitaker rode with Faith Christine. Faith Christine had decided who went in which car, which is why I got to have Charles in my truck.

Charles hurried ahead and was waiting for me outside my truck when I left the gravesite. He got into the passenger side of my Ford, his face noncommittal. I should be able to pump him for information. That was what Faith Christine had probably planned. Instead, he said abruptly, "Well, that's over."

I was a little startled, but I said, "Right."

The truth was, I didn't know how to start and he wasn't talkative, either, to say the least.

He never looked over at me once, as I backed out of the parking space and drove out onto the main road. He stared out the window of the cab on his side of the truck as if it was the first time he had seen each mile of dirt and it was the most fascinating dirt he'd ever seen. Obviously he would have rather ridden with Faith Christine and Miss Whitaker.

After five minutes of silence, I wished the same thing. Finally I asked, "What is Miss Whitaker's first name?"

He said dully, "Jan."

Then he added a few moments later, "But I can't call her that." She was obviously supposed to keep her professional distance.

"But she seems to like you," I said.

"I like her, too." he said.

"It was nice of her to come up here both times with you," I said.

"It's her job," he said again noncommittally.

It was my impression that she was interested in Charles more than as just her job, but that was not my place to say. They'd have to work that out by themselves. I knew that they weren't supposed to get emotionally involved.

Silence. For a long time. We were halfway to Faith Christine's, and I hadn't gotten anywhere with Charles. Is this the time? If I didn't make my best attempt now to reach him, it might be too late, later.

"Charles," I said, "I'm going to be perfectly honest with you—"

"Well, that would be a refreshing change," he said abruptly.

Did he mean me? That he didn't trust me any more than the bunch of—to be honest—liars he had had to deal with?

Then he said, "I didn't mean that the way it sounded. I have no reason not to trust you. You seem to be one of the good guys, but . . ."

I shook my head in understanding of his situation.

"I want to talk to you about some of those things—the

things that have happened to you in your life," I said suddenly, before I even consciously made a decision. I pulled off in the dirt at the side of the road, and turned off the engine.

No other cars were in sight.

This was as good a place as any to state my case.

"We need to talk," I said. "I'm going to lay all my cards on the table. I'm not good at pussyfooting."

He rolled down the window, as if he needed air. I was watching for any sign that he was uncomfortable, was resenting this talk, or was disturbed that I had pulled off the road to talk. He gave me no indication, either way. His attitude was that he couldn't care less.

But I did.

So I plunged in.

"I have learned . . . some information," I said stupidly and awkwardly, resisting the urge at the last second to call it "startling information," as I unrolled the window on my side of the cab, too. "Since your father's death. Information about your—" Here I had to plunge in. "—birth."

He nodded, still looking out the window and not at me.

I did not take this as a good sign.

"Were you aware that you were adopted?" I asked.

He turned and looked out the front windshield now. It was a slight improvement, and gave me a little hope.

"Yeah." His "yeah" was a word full of emotions, complex and not pleasant. His was not one of the successful adoptions that you hear about on TV, I gathered.

"How did you feel about Oldman and Jessica?" I said.

"What was there to feel?" he said bitterly. "She croaked right away, and he never gave a damn about Beth and me. He never really wanted us. It was just something she insisted on, from what I hear. She *always* got her own way. A Class One, Grade A manipulator. Used her illness and/ or her money to get what she wanted."

"I'm sorry," I said.

"Hey, it's all right. It's cool. It's all in the past," he said. "Start off each day new, one day at a time—all that stuff," he said, I thought, too bitterly to be really meaning it.

It wasn't all right. I said so.

He looked startled, but he looked over at me, into my eyes, for the first time. Like he was really seeing me for the first time. The look was intense and piercing.

It was hard to look at his eyes and not stare at the three rings piercing his brow. Didn't that hurt? *How do you sleep with those ugly things hanging there?* I wanted to ask.

Instead, I had to get to the point before I lost his attention and concentration.

"I have to make a hard decision here," I said. "And I don't know if I'm doing the right thing." Especially here on the road, when Miss Whitaker was on her way to Faith Christine's and not available.

But I felt my best chance to get his attention was now. It was gut feeling more than anything else.

"I could not say anything to you, and your life could go on pretty much the same way as it is now . . ." Meaning that he was trying to get help. "But I feel that I owe you honesty, and the truth." I gripped the steering wheel with both hands. Maybe I'd ease into it bit by bit. Then I could stop if it seemed to be too much for him, at any point.

"I came upon some information as I was going through some legal papers," I said.

"What about?" he said, seeming really interested, and

still paying attention. He'd somewhat lost his slouch, his disinterest, and his disdainful attitude.

"Your adoption papers."

"What about them?"

Still pussyfooting. Get to the point: "I didn't like the looks of them."

He perked up, and seemed almost pleased.

"How? How didn't you like the looks of them?" he said.

I was a little surprised. I'd thought he'd be angry, or worried.

Instead he seemed pleased.

"I always wondered, like a lot of adopted kids, why my parents—my biological parents—gave me up. Why didn't they love me and want to keep me? How can parents give away a child?" he asked in a rhetorical way.

"Why did they give me away? Was I that unlovable?" he asked, looking out the window on his side again, but this time I suspected that it was to not let me see him cry.

Was that why he had looked out the window before?

Now I sensed that I had a wonderful gift to give this forlorn young man: this conversation was going a lot better than I expected, and in a way I hadn't suspected it would go.

"Well," I said very slowly, so as not to screw things up, "I can lay your worries to rest about being unlovable. What I am trying to tell you is that it appears your biological parents did not give you up," I said carefully. "You might have been stolen from your biological parents."

When I said the word "stolen," it was as if a light went on in his face. And sadness disappeared from his eyes. I could tell a great weight had been lifted from him.

I could understand how he felt; he'd just said that he felt

his original parents had rejected him; and then Jessica died and then Oldman had not appeared to want him either.

What a series of blows—first your parents don't want you, and then neither does your one surviving adoptive parent. No wonder Charles was bitter.

But I was not above getting a word in here regarding soberness—sobriety—as a goal.

"If you want to begin looking for your biological parents—and there's no guarantee that you and I can even find them after all this time—I would hope that you can see that if they have already been through years of suffering from your disappearance, that the least you can do is try to return to them clean and sober—drug-free.

"I can only guess how bad they would feel if they finally found you after all these years—" I decided not to pull my punch "—and find out you are a substance abuser."

He leaned over and hugged me, evidently not holding my blunt talk against me.

"Let's go," he said. "I've got to tell Jan—that is, Miss Whitaker!"

I turned on the key, pulled back onto the road, and we drove off. I decided to press my luck.

"I've been trying to get a hold of Beth," I said, casually. "Do you have a photo of her?"

He didn't bite. He was obviously running through his mind the news I'd just told him. He didn't seem to even hear me.

But I was encouraged by the look on his face when I had said the anti-drug thing. He seemed to agree that his biological parents at least deserved that.

He was sitting up straighter in his seat.

I didn't want to spoil his euphoria, but I had to give him

a word of warning: "There's no guarantee that we can find them, or that they'll be nice people when—and if—we do," I said.

"Don't you see," he said, looking joyfully at me, "that that really doesn't matter? It's the fact that they didn't give me up—they wanted me—that matters. That changes everything. My whole life—that changes everything."

He was right. He had gone from believing all his life that nobody wanted him, to a totally different truthful reality where his parents wanted him, and his adoptive parents also wanted him enough to buy a stolen baby.

"I don't have a photo of Beth," he said, finally.

As I continued on to Faith Christine's, I filled him in about the baby-stealing ring of Mrs. Simpson-Getts of Nevada.

"You know what's funny about what you're saying?" Charles said. "I always thought I remembered seeing palm trees, blue water, and a real big, real old stone-wall fort with low walls next to the water when I was little. Everyone always told me I was crazy."

"It sounds to me like a description of St. Augustine, Florida. We'll have to check on that," I said.

Chapter Sixteen

Sometimes I know when to shut up, and I knew that pressing Charles for information right at this moment about Beth was useless; he was too preoccupied with his good news.

Later, I could try again, or have Faith Christine try again. I had to talk to him about financial matters—legal things— but I could wait until I knew more about things for that. He might even know more than I did, right now.

I wondered if Beth would be as happy about the news of her adoption. Charles had never asked if Beth was stolen. Not a close family, to say the least. Later, maybe he'd have more questions.

When we pulled into the driveway and parked, he gave me a quick, emotional hug—a kind of a thank-you—and jumped out of the truck to go in search of Jan Whitaker.

Faith Christine came out of the house, and met me on

her porch. We sat. Just a few people were wandering about, parking and going into the house. We nodded and greeted one or two, and directed them inside to the food, which some church ladies had stayed at Faith Christine's to prepare instead of attending the service for Oldman.

She smiled at me. "Glad it's over?" she said.

"Told Charles about the illegal adoption," I said.

"I guessed as much," she said, smiling at me.

"He was thrilled." I didn't add the truth, that it was not the reaction I expected.

"Of course he was thrilled, silly," she said. "Wouldn't you be?"

In a few minutes we went inside and I made myself a giant roast beef sandwich from the food that the women had put out. After that I had some potato salad and then a big piece of homemade chocolate cake. Faith Christine was busy helping everyone, making more coffee and doing things in the kitchen.

No alcohol was served because of Charles.

Jerry sidled up to me and whispered, "I could use a stiff drink." He was only half-serious, because he considered himself on duty.

"I told Charles about the adoption," I said.

"I know. He mentioned it to me, as did a half a dozen other people."

"You liar," I said jokingly. "There's not half a dozen people here."

We looked. I was wrong.

Now there were about two dozen people here, more than were at the funeral service and the gravesite. They had just sort of drifted in without my noticing in the last few minutes. He understood my surprise. "Came for Faith

Christine's food spread," he said, "just like me." He leaned close to my ear. "You always eat this good at Faith Christine's?"

I nodded my head yes.

"Lucky dog," he joked back, then he walked away to talk to someone who had just come in.

I wandered toward the door. Patricia was still with Peter, who had driven her to the funeral and back here. She was considered out of danger, but Peter was stuck to her side like glue. They were in the house on the couch sitting side by side as I passed.

I went outside.

Ditto Ken and Arlene, but outside, by the mule corral.

Two romances. No, three. No, four. Pat and Peter, Faith Christine and me, Ken and Arlene, and the forbidden one of Charles and Jan Whitaker.

Where was Beth? Did I have to search every homeless shelter from here to Los Angeles? Was she hiding because she was the murderer?

Should I wait until tomorrow, or go over to Oldman's house later today? I'd have to get permission from Jerry, but I didn't think I'd have any trouble getting it. I should have mentioned it when I talked to him a few minutes ago. They should be completely through there, at Oldman's.

I didn't feel like talking much to anybody, so I went around to the back of the house. Keeping out of sight from anybody looking out the picture window in her kitchen, I sat on the ground, looking at the mountain.

From here you could see the trail that the mules took to the mountain.

On my ranch, it was horse tracks that made the trail. Sometimes Faith Christine and I took rides on Spot and

Patches, my two Appaloosas. They were pretty self-sufficient in the summer. They had water in their pasture and a lot of land to graze on. Peter and Pat took a short ride yesterday, they'd told me; the horses had had exercise, a good brushing, and some grain.

I was taking a lot for granted. I was calling her Pat already in my mind.

I heard someone behind me, and Miss Whitaker appeared at my side. She was wearing high heels, and a pretty pale-green, very loose dress that hung to her ankles. Dangling earrings with a pearl that hung at the bottoms of gold zig-zags.

She sat right down on the dirt next to me. "Chuck told me what you told him earlier," she said. "It's made him very happy," she added.

"I just don't want him to get disappointed," I said. "Even if we did find his birth parents, they could be creeps, or bums."

"He's aware of that."

"I can't quite get the hang of you," I said in what I hoped was my most pleasant voice, smiling down at her. "You're such a dainty little thing and look so young, but you have a job that would scare the . . . whatever out of me. Such responsibility, and it doesn't seem to bother you."

She looked at me without smiling, and it made her look older. "It bothers me, all right. Sometimes I can't sleep nights, worrying. But I tell myself someone has to do it, and I do the best I can."

"What about Charles?" I asked. "You seem to like each other very much; but I know there must be rules about that. There are rules, aren't there?"

She bit her lip. I was right; she had thought about a

relationship. "One day at a time," she said. "One thing at a time." That was all I could get out of her.

"Well, I know I'm too old-fashioned, but I'm just old enough to hate shaved heads. They have a bad"—I searched for the right word—"connotation," I finally said, "with my age group. It's about as popular as having KKK on your license plate." I looked at her. "Frankly, I think it's scary." She drew straight lines in the sandy dirt in front of her with the finger next to her thumb. Her fingernail was painted with green nail polish that matched her dress.

My guess was that she was about twenty-five or twenty-six. Younger than Chuck. "He doesn't mean anything by it," she said. "He's being overtly rebellious. He's really a nice, shy person."

Overtly rebellious. College talk. Psychology class.

"Not violent at all, in your opinion?"

"In my opinion, for what it's worth, no."

At least she didn't say "acting out."

My hiding place having been discovered, I got up when she got up, and we went around back to the front of the house and I sat on the porch. She went inside, presumably to find Chuck. The front window in back of the rocking chair was open, and I could hear two little old church ladies (they must have been in their mid-seventies) inside the house in the living room, complaining about the weather. ". . . and it's so hot at noon I have to search for a tree to stand under, but at night I have to put on a blanket," one said benignly. Used to it, but didn't like it, I gathered.

"I forgot what I was saying," one lady said. "What were we talking about before I got side-tracked onto the weather?"

"You were talking about the angel watching. . . ."

I tried to block the talk out; I hate this current guardian angel stuff the wackos have latched onto recently. I had noticed that a couple of church ladies had tiny gold guardian angel pins on their dress or suit lapels at the funeral service. If you wear one your guardian angel is supposed to watch out for you.

"Yes. Oh, yes. Well, it was weird, I tell you. I didn't like it one bit."

Good for you, old mama.

Enough of unintentional eavesdropping.

I got up and went over to look at the mules. I rested my arms over one of the top poles of the corral. Peace and quiet. The three mules out of the barn were standing on the far side of the corral.

Five minutes later a little old church lady brushed up against my side, she was so close. She barely came up to my elbow. Gray hair and gray dress with a white collar and cuffs.

"Oh, excuse me," she said.

"No problem."

"Somebody inside told me you could help me," she whispered. She spoke in a humble sad way, as if I were God. I hate that.

"Who?" I whispered back.

She ignored that and continued. "She said that you might be able to help me with my . . . problem."

Guess who.

Free legal advice at social events.

My favorite thing.

Thanks, Faith Christine.

"What is it," I said to the grandmotherly-looking woman standing next to me, whispering confidentially.

"Well, a couple of years ago my husband died," she began. "And, well, on his deathbed, he made me promise something. And now, I . . . met someone."

"He made you promise that you wouldn't marry again?"

"Yes."

"Well," I said, "let me tell you what *I* think about deathbed promises. First, it's not a good thing for a dying person to do to another person, even with the best intentions. The guilt would be tremendous if you refused. The dying person knows that. Therefore, in my opinion," I continued, "a deathbed promise is a manipulative thing to do; that person is *still* trying to control you from the grave."

She bobbed her head in agreement. She was listening intently to what I was saying.

"You don't owe a person that. They were wrong to ask it of you. Some people find it helpful to go to the grave site, and have a talk with the deceased, so to speak. Say, 'I'm sorry, George—or whatever his name is—but I can't keep my promise to you any longer.' And tell him why. Tell him it was wrong of him to ask you to make a promise like that. I think you can figure out the rest of what to say."

She grabbed one of my hands with both of her small hands and pumped it up and down. Many, many times.

Then she hurriedly left. As I turned to watch her go, I saw a tiny but dapper old man waiting for her, looking worried, on Faith Christine's porch. She went up to him and he put his arm around her, comforting her tears of relief. Together, they went back in the house. Make that five romances at Faith Christine's house today.

Faith Christine slipped up beside me.

"How did it go with Mrs. Webster?" she asked softly.

"Okay."

"What did you tell her?"

"The truth."

"And that is . . ."

"It's wrong for a dying person to use their death to extract a promise. It takes away the living person's ability to make their own decisions in life, and that's wrong."

"You told her that?"

"I told her to go and 'have a talk' with her deceased husband and tell him that she's decided not to honor her promise any longer. He had no right to manipulate her like that."

"She wants to marry Mr. Brady. He's a nice man. So are you," she said, slipping her arm through mine and walking me back toward the house.

"Well, I heard her earlier saying that she didn't like that guardian angel stuff either, and I figured that she couldn't be all bad," I said jokingly. "I need a cup of coffee. Is there any left inside?"

She nodded.

"By the way," I said, "you went out to visit Esther Cooper the other day. How is she doing? I saw her at the church and the cemetery, but she didn't come to the house." I didn't add that the woman looked a lot more disheveled than usual at the church and at the cemetery. Her salt-and-pepper hair was in disarray and her green-and-white flowered dress looked soiled in spots.

She was silent, which was unlike Faith Christine. I wondered what it was that was keeping her silent on the subject of the egg lady. Faith Christine was looking very guilty. "I—I'm afraid I asked Peter to run her name through his computer. I don't know . . ." Her voice trailed off. I could tell she was torn. Loyalty to the egg lady Esther Cooper, or something else? Was there something more sinister about Esther Cooper than I realized? What was Faith Christine holding back?

I couldn't force her to tell me. So I waited. If she was ready, when she was ready, she would tell me.

I could see she was struggling with herself.

"There's been two murders," I gently reminded her.

"I know," she said. "I know." She sighed. "When I went to visit Esther, the day after Oldman's murder, I had to use the bathroom. When I went into the bathroom, I saw blood on a sweater sitting there. I know it was her sweater, because I've seen her wearing it. It was around the bottom of the sleeves. I feel guilty telling you this, like I went to spy on her or something, but I really had to use the bathroom—"

I put my arm around Faith Christine. "It's all right."

"I've been so worried. I didn't know whether to tell anyone or not. And Esther would know it was me who told. I don't think she'd murder anyone, but—"

"Don't worry about it. Jerry can go and check it out without letting on you told. There's probably some innocent explanation. And she did find the body."

"That's just what worries me. If the police had seen the blood on her sweater then, they would have confiscated that sweater. The fact that they didn't—if she hid the fact that she had gotten blood on herself—"

"I see what you mean," I said.

"Nobody knows how long she was in that house before she reported the murder. We only have her word for what happened, and when she arrived. Up until I saw that blood, I never doubted her story. I was sorry for her, that's why I went over there. The truth is, she keeps pretty much to herself, and we don't know anything about her; her past, and even where she came from before she moved here. She just appeared here about ten years ago, bought chickens, and became 'the egg lady.' "

"I know."

"You better tell Jerry what you know."

She nodded, moving away from my arms and looking up at me regretfully. "All right," she said. "I'll go find Jerry." She looked up at me, then walked back to the house.

A few minutes later, I saw her come out of the house with Jerry. The two of them walked down the driveway away from everybody and I could see them talking intently.

As they walked back a few minutes later, Jerry nodded to me as they passed. Faith Christine looked as if she had been crying. She didn't like to be the one to get anyone in trouble, especially a little old lady who lived close by.

But crazy murderers come in all shapes and sizes, and it couldn't hurt to check, even on the egg lady.

Chapter Seventeen

It was close to four o'clock. Jerry wandered over to where I was sitting on the porch; beat, my kids would say "to the max." The windows behind us were closed; no one could hear what we were saying if we kept our voices down.

Almost everyone was gone, except for a few stragglers and the people staying with either Faith Christine or myself.

"Well, as a help, this funeral has been a bust, except for the tip about Esther Cooper's bloody sweater," Jerry said. "We're working on seeing if she is who she says she is."

"What about the bloody sweater?"

"I'm going over there to see if I can locate it. I can have to pee, too, when I visit someone. She probably got blood on herself when she discovered the body, but she was *not* wearing a sweater when I arrived at the scene. She might have gotten scared to have blood on her and put it in the trunk of her car so we wouldn't see it. And she may have

145

washed it by now. Although Faith Christine says that to save water, Esther does laundry once a week. She's done that for years, according to Faith Christine. And old, ingrained habits die hard in some people."

"Even if the sweater has Oldman Reilly's blood on it?"

He shook his head. "Nothing people do surprises me. If I find the sweater, I'll just ask her about it first."

"It's worth a try," I said.

"How did you make out talking to Charles Reilly?"

"Better than I expected," I admitted.

"Well, I asked him point-blank; do you think Beth is capable of murder?" Jerry said, as he sat down in one of the other chairs.

"What did he say?" I asked.

"Nothing. Nada. Zip. I can't get through to him. From his attitude, I get the feeling that he doesn't like her much." He stroked his chin. "Not much—if any—real affection there."

"That's understandable, under the circumstances."

"Yeah, I guess. He draws the line at actually saying that she's capable of murder."

"So does Faith Christine," I said.

"Miss Whitaker says that he's rebellious, and you're an authority figure, so don't take his uncooperativeness too personally," I added.

"I don't, but time is running out. We haven't been able to find Beth. The paper trail ends two years ago."

I told him about the letter I had from the homeless place in Los Angeles; we walked out to my truck, and I gave him the letter. I locked the papers back up, and we walked back to the porch and sat.

"Perpetual Humility?" he said, making a comical face in

disbelief at the name. He waved the paper. "I'll check on this. We have a couple of prints we haven't been able to identify, and we don't have Beth's fingerprints, anyway."

"Any on Oldman's truck?"

"No."

"Whoever did it walked in from a parking place outside the property we haven't been able to find, or came in their own vehicle, is my guess. Maybe parked on the asphalt. No car or truck tracks in the yard are any help—you know what the dirt is like up here. Wind doesn't help, either."

"If it's all right with you, tomorrow I'd like to go through Oldman's papers and things—in my capacity as his executor," I said.

"I can't see anything wrong with that," Jerry said.

"You want me to wear plastic fingers and booties again?" I asked.

"Yes. If you don't mind. In fact, if you don't mind, I'd like to go with you."

"That's fine. What time?" I asked, aware that his schedule was more complex than mine.

"Two," he said. "Two would be good for me."

"By the way, I was wondering if Charles has been totally eliminated as a suspect. I know he was supposed to be in rehab at the time of his father's murder. Did anybody check on that?"

"He was in sight of somebody from the rehab way before both murders until way after. Lots of witnesses." He chuckled. "From what I can see, he's rarely out of Miss Whitaker's sight. Too bad that a relationship would be unethical right now. But she seems like a decent person. If we need to, we can ask him to take a lie detector test; but he doesn't seem the type to hire a killer. He's benefiting by his mother's money, so why kill Oldman? It's his mother who had the money."

"Did you ever find out what his fight with Beth was about two years ago?"

Jerry ran his hand over his hair. "It was pretty much over nothing. Charles misplaced his wallet and thought that maybe Beth had swiped it. He found it, right where he had left it, after she left. He says he always felt a little guilty about Beth after that. He admits he and Beth were never close. He was embarrassed as a teenager, by her 'weird-ness' as he calls it, in front of his friends."

I was tired and wanted this day to be over.

But one small significant thing happened. Just before he left to return to rehab in Los Angeles, Charles gathered his things and came over to where I was standing, and said good-bye. The small but significant thing was that the three gold rings were gone from his eyebrow.

When I went into the bathroom a few minutes later, I saw the three eyebrow rings. They were in the wastebasket. I held up my arm in a clenched fist and said, "Yes!"

A few minutes later, I said my good-byes, and drove home. Peter would be along later. That was fine with me. He still hadn't mentioned moving back in with me.

Tomorrow, he would probably be returning home to Los Angeles, and back to his job, I guessed. He'd only men-tioned staying until the funeral.

Which reminded me. In a few days, I would be attending George Finley's funeral to see who came. My hope was fading that the murderer would attend that one if they didn't attend today's funeral. Or did they? Was the murderer at the funeral and I just didn't recognize him or her as such? Was I missing seeing something?

Esther Cooper, the egg lady, who had found Oldman Reilly's body, was now on the list of people to be looked at more closely.

I could hardly visualize any of the people attending the events today hacking at an old man with a knife. Then later, hacking at a lawyer.

Well, okay, the lawyer I could understand, I joked to myself.

I pulled into my driveway.

Didn't I leave my shades up? Dora and I both hated blinds. I know it's old-fashioned, but I still used shades, although they are getting harder and harder to find when I need new ones.

The shades were down on the three windows facing me on the front of the house: the living room, and the two bedrooms up the hall on the front side.

Peter never moved a shade, and besides, I was the last to leave the house. And the first home, I was sure.

No vehicles parked anywhere. No strange vehicle tracks.

I made a quick right, and pulled in to park beside the barn, out of sight of the house. Shutting off the engine, I didn't pocket my keys but held them tightly in my hand so that they didn't make any sound.

Then I quietly walked toward the house, feeling like a gunslinger of the Old West, watching everywhere.

Incongruously, I thought of the Great Dane. Maybe I should get one.

Reaching the porch and the door, I quietly tried the handle. My heart started pounding a little louder than usual, and I thought, *I'm too old for this!*

The door was still locked.

I said "phew" to myself, then I noticed that the living

room window—with the shade down—was *entirely* empty. No glass. Someone had gotten in by breaking a window and climbing through.

Easy as pie to do standing on my porch, and one of the reasons that, before the murders, I never bothered to lock the door. It had been pretty safe here prior to the murders.

All I had gone and done by locking the house was go and get my window broken. The buggers had dropped the glass inside the house, I bet, although now that I looked close, there were a few tiny shards of glass glittering on the floor of the porch.

My keys always make noise as they turn the lock and I didn't want to alert the intruder, so I crept over and began to ease myself—not an easy job because my arms and legs are long—through the open window. The couch was right in front of the window. Climbing through that window and over the back of the couch was not easy, at my age. I had to resist openly groaning as I pulled myself in and then twisted and contorted my body to get my legs in and not fall off the couch in the process, or get cut by broken glass.

The rest of the windows—the ones not on the porch— on the other three sides of the house were up off the ground sufficiently so that no one could get in that way without a stepladder.

As I carefully put the keys quietly down on the end table next to the sofa, I looked around. The living room was not trashed. Not at all. Nothing looked the least out of place except for broken glass.

The big question was, was the murderer still here?

I was well aware that the person was a silent attacker—a knife-wielder. I'd better be careful.

Don't turn your back on any open doorways.

I headed across the living room to my hallway. I'd never been scared to walk around in my own house before, but visualizing what Oldman and the lawyer looked like was enough to make me careful.

My plan was to get to the room at the end of the hall which used to be the girls' bedroom. It was now used as my office.

To do this, I had to pass the bathroom door on the left and two more doorways to bedrooms. The second bedroom doorway was directly opposite my office door at the end of the hall.

I reached the bathroom door first, and gently pushed it back with my left hand; all clear in there. The sink and toilet were on the left, and the bathtub on the right. I moved inside just enough to see that no one was hiding in the bathtub.

Creeping silently back into the hall, I had both my hands up in front of me in case a knife came at me, and proceeded down the hallway. I peered cautiously into the first bedroom on the right, and into the closet. This was Peter's room. A platform bed; no way to hide under it. His closet was so stuffed with electronic stuff that a toad couldn't hide inside it. An old computer was in the corner.

Out in the hall again, I looked into the end bedroom on the left. My bedroom.

No one in there. I checked under the bed and there was nothing there but my slippers and a bunch of my shoes and a little dust. Okay, a lot of dust.

Closet okay. Well, not okay, a mess. But nobody in there. Dora's side pretty much empty. I had given her clothing to the Salvation Army Thrift Store in Rushing River Junction six months after her death.

I was beginning to feel very foolish for having been so worried. I had to remind myself again what Oldman and George looked like.

Across the hall, and here was the mess.

Papers all over the place, moved around, disturbed, but oddly enough, still stacked in piles according to what they were about.

So the killer was still around. Maybe not here, now, but still in the area. I didn't bother to look to see what was missing—good luck to the intruder if they thought that I had any papers worth stealing in there. I didn't.

All the accumulated papers about Oldman and his family and the maroon folder were still locked in my truck. I had been running back and forth so much to Faith Christine's, it was easier to just keep them with me. They hadn't been very helpful anyway.

There was one thing that the intruder had left behind. There was a note in the center of my desk. In block letters on a plain sheet of paper face up, it said:

MIND YOUR OWN BUSINESS
OR YOU COULD END UP DEAD
LIKE THE REST OF THEM

I grabbed the phone and called the police. Jerry wasn't there, the dispatcher said, but he'd get in touch with him; he was sure that Jerry would be out right away.

I checked the rest of the house then went back to my office. I thought I'd take a closer look and see if anything was missing. Nothing. I checked my sock drawer for my cash stash. No money missing.

I checked for other valuables while I was waiting for

Jerry. Nothing gone that I could see. A lawyer, and I didn't have a list of the valuables I own. What a jerk.

The doorbell rang. It was Jerry. I could see another police cruiser coming in the driveway and parking. I let Jerry in, and showed him the note. He put on plastic gloves, picked up the note, and sealed it in a Baggie.

"Did you touch it?"

"No."

"Is it written on your paper?"

"No. I don't own any notepaper like that."

"Good." Jerry said.

We waited by the door for the other policeman, whose name badge said Richard Brown. I was unfamiliar with this officer. He was quiet and just listened.

The intruder was neat, I told Jerry. "A man would have made more of a mess, looking," I said.

"Uh-oh," Jerry said. "The Women's Rights Movement wouldn't like to hear you make an assumption like that," he said, trying to lighten the mood. He turned serious. "But a pro wouldn't," he said. "And I'll send a guy out here to check, but my guess is that there won't be any fingerprints on the glass, either. Or on your desk. Every weenie in America knows enough to wear gloves on a break-in."

"I thought you called them B and E's. Breaking and Entering," I said.

"You watch too much TV," he said.

I told him how the shades had alerted me that something was wrong.

"It seems foolish and unnecessary to put down the shades way out here, where there would be very slim chance of anyone seeing in the windows during the day when it was bright outside and darker in the house," Jerry said.

"Something a city person would do out of habit?" Richard Brown volunteered.

"I'll have the fingerprint guy come over," Jerry said, smiling. "Doesn't that sound important? It's Bubba. Anyway, I'll have him do the shades, too."

Bubba? A Bubba in Northern California?

"Have them check the toilet," I said, on a hunch. "It's a long way out here, and a woman might have to go."

"Beth?"

"I don't know. My wife, my daughters and Faith Christine always seem to have to use the bathroom when we get home. And ladies don't like to pee with gloves on. It's worth a try."

"I'm desperate. I'll try anything."

Richard Brown stood there, not quite knowing how to take the bantering back and forth between Jerry and me. I could see that it made him uncomfortable.

Outside, we found a few heel marks in the dirt, made by what looked like the heel of medium-sized western-style boot. Not a clear print of the front part of the boot; the wind had blown that away. Three other policemen arrived. It seemed they were mostly standing around chatting, although they were discussing things about the case from time to time.

I used to get mad at cops when they don't seem to be actively doing anything. When they're standing around. But then I say to myself, *You don't have to be actively doing anything to be working on something. You can be working in your brain.*

I'm the last person who should be criticizing anyone for doing that; I remembered "taciturn" and "reticent."

I also remembered my reasons twenty years ago, for giving up an occupation that had brought Dora and me a lot of money. A *lot* of money. But it came with stress, a lot of stress, just like a cops's job. Dealing with the cruelty and back-stabbing and ruthlessness of takeovers and cut-throat mergers had taken its toll on me.

By my early thirties, somewhat like a police officer, I had seen one too many nasty human beings and gotten bitter and cynical. Dora didn't like it. It was then that Dora and I made the drastic change to ranching in this beautiful rugged area of mountains, pastureland, and pines. The kids loved it, too. Especially the chance to own horses.

Peter walked in the door, looking worried. I told him what happened. He looked around, and satisfied that I was temporarily safe, went out and put the horses in the barn. I owed him. He'd been a big help lately.

Jerry took me aside and he said that he'd been out to Esther Cooper's house and found the sweater. Esther had been upset, he said, but insisted that the blood on the sweater was hers. Jerry was sending the sweater to the lab to find out. Esther didn't have a problem with him taking the sweater to be tested.

"She's a real weird lady," Jerry said. "Really weird. Lives in a house that's full of stuff. You can hardly walk from room to room; she's got piles of useless stuff like newspapers and magazines. I'm a neat-freak, compared to her. I couldn't stand living in a house like that," Jerry said.

"I've never been inside her house," I said. "She delivers eggs to me, but I send her a check once a month."

"We'll know more about her by tomorrow morning. I've got guys working on it."

Finally Jerry and the other policemen left. It had been a long day.

I was glad to get into bed. I was glad Peter was home, sleeping down the hall; but at the same time, I was worried that he was home.

I didn't sleep well. I was awake, listening almost the whole night for the intruder's return.

I was worrying about that note.

Chapter Eighteen

I got up at dawn, and went out and saddled up Spot. I
needed to get away for a while.

Taking nothing but my very rusty gold pan, a small plastic bag and a tweezers, I rode up to where I liked to pan
for gold. For July, it was an abnormally gray, cold day.

The morning sun hadn't warmed up the earth yet, so I
was glad that I had on my old brown leather vest.

I rode Spot to my secret place. The fancy name for it
was an "alluvial plain." The shape of the ancient river bed
was there, in the dirt, if you looked carefully, and knew
what you were looking for. Now, only a tiny stream re-
mained, which sometimes dried up.

Today, it was there; I didn't have to dry pan.

I picketed Spot, after letting him drink.

Because I hadn't brought a shovel, I used my pan to dig
down near the far edge of the ancient riverbed, where the

gold would have been deposited during a time of fast-moving water, and brought the sand, which had small grains of black sand in it, to the edge of the stream and began panning for gold. The water here is always pretty cold, but in July it's closest to the warmest it ever gets.

Black sand is always a good indication of gold.

I squatted, and tipped the pan under the water carefully, and then began the circling motion with my wrists.

When I was done, the gold was there, at the bottom of my pan in a neat semi-circle, separated as if by magic (the magic of experienced wrist-motion) from the black sand next to it. There were five small grains of gold in this particular pan.

Anyone who has done it knows that it is real hard work, panning for gold. Each pan takes quite a while, especially if you are a beginner. A beginner might take half an hour; it took me about two minutes for each pan.

Something for nothing except for back-breaking work. The American dream in a nutshell.

In a couple of hours I had a backache and a little gold dust—nothing to shout about, but satisfying. I felt a little more at peace. Less stressed. It was beautiful here. The clouds that had made the sky gray were clearing off, it was already warming up, and the sun was getting ready to come back out, I thought.

With tweezers, I'd picked out each gold speck and put it into the tiniest size plastic zip-lock type bag, and tucked it into my pocket. At home, I would pour these few grains into another plastic bag I kept in one of my socks in my sock drawer. Peter called it "gold rocks in my socks." The truth was, they were minute flakes of gold.

I never did anything with my gold; just kept it, there in

my sock. There wasn't a giant amount. I had no idea of how much it was worth. I'd never had it weighed to find out. I didn't want to sell it. Just hoarded twenty years worth of small gold flakes. A couple of small nuggets.

Last night, I'd checked on it while waiting for Jerry. Still there.

I looked at my watch; quarter-to-eight. I was hungry, and I had to take care of the horses. I rode back home. I patted Spot on his neck as I rode. He was a good friend.

Back home, I did my chores (shoveled the manure out of the barn), tended the horses, checked on the cattle and went in the house.

Peter had pancakes ready. I ate a stack dripping with margarine and syrup; more than I should have.

"I'm meeting Jerry at two," I said as I ate.

"Dad, I'm thinking of moving back to Rushing River Junction," Peter said, sipping his coffee.

"I think that that will be great," I said.

"As soon as I can," he said.

"Faith Christine told me about your 'decentralization,' " I said.

I told him about the letter I'd received from the lady who ran the homeless shelter and told him how I gave it to Jerry. "Thanks for your help, Peter," I said.

"When I get back to Los Angeles I'll go and talk to the lady at Our Lady of Perpetual Humility and find out what I can for you about Beth," he said.

"That will be very helpful," I said. "Before I go to Old-man's today, I was thinking of taking a ride down to Tranquility House."

"I meant to tell you, Dad, I saw it on the eleven o'clock

news last night about Heal the Breach. Your name wasn't mentioned."

"Good."

I didn't want to upset the people of Tranquility House before I got a chance to talk to them.

"By the way, Dad. I hope you don't mind. I called the glass company in Rushing River Junction, and they are sending somebody out to fix the window. They said they'll mail you the bill if you're not home when they come to do it."

"Mary's Glass?"

"Yes."

"Fine. They do a good job."

Peter grinned. "I know, I know." He was jokingly referring to the times that softballs had come through the windows when he was growing up.

He cleaned up his breakfast things, made his bed, and left for Los Angeles.

I did the same for my own things, and left for Tranquility House, arriving there at ten-thirty.

Tranquility House was different from the first two places I had been. Privately owned, it looked like a Spanish mission.

"Only twenty-five patients," Miss Paternoster told me. "We strive for a family atmosphere," she said in a voice so perfected I couldn't tell whether it was a real friendly or a fake friendly voice, and I pride myself on that.

Okay, maybe half and half. I got right to the point.

"I don't know if you've read in the papers about Oldman Reilly's death," I said.

"Oh, my dear, yes. Yes," she said.

I am not her dear. I ignored that. She lost one point.

"I am Mr. Oldman's executor—"

I needed to say no more. Either she sensed possible mention in his will, or the return of Beth to their facility—I didn't know, but she was as syrupy-sweet as my pancakes had been that morning.

"We *loved* Beth, you know," she oozed.

I nodded as if in sympathy.

"What exactly caused her to leave?" I oozed back, as if shocked at the entire prospect of that ever happening.

She looked around as if it were entirely possible that anyone must be mad to consider leaving. She used her hand to flip her long brown hair away from her neck, sending her long silver earrings in the shape of a mobile with the sun, moon, and stars circling wildly in tiny orbits around her earlobes.

"A . . . relationship developed." she said cautiously.

She adjusted the neckline of the red, yellow, white, and black Mexican peasant-style blouse she wore.

She indicated disapproval; a slight wrinkle of her nose. "We did our best to break it up, of course," she said delicately; fingering her sterling silver pinky ring.

"It was . . . well, we discourage any relationships here between . . ." she paused. "But—"

It was a big but. Like you can't help it if they sneak.

"Particularly ones we consider . . . not beneficial. Of course, we did *all* we could. . . ." she trailed off.

"I see," I said, beginning to understand.

"Linda had even more problems than—"

Oh, boy.

Than Beth. Who heard voices. Who thought God was talking to her.

"They ran away, in the end," she finished sadly. "Of

course, we'd be glad to take *Beth* back," she added, clearly meaning that she wouldn't touch Linda with a ten-foot pole.

"I notified Oldman, of course, and he did his best to find her—them," she said, fingering her gazillion silver bracelets, untangling them and separating them neatly into rings around her lower arm.

No wonder Charles was not happy. No wonder he was angry at his sister. Maybe because she was running around with a woman with worse problems than Beth's. Chances are—were—that neither one was taking their medications.

"I don't have a clue where they might be," Miss Paternoster said. "This all happened two years ago. And don't forget, Beth was over twenty-one."

"She was visiting a shelter for the homeless in Los Angeles off and on, until two months ago," I said.

"Oh, dear," she said.

"I wonder if you could tell me Linda's last name," I said. "So I could ask the woman at the homeless shelter if they were together or not."

"Oh, certainly," Miss Paternoster said. "Linda Pavell—one v, two ll's."

I thanked her. She had sincerely tried to help. Seemed like a nice person. She wasn't giving away anything confidential because evidently the friendship was common knowledge. She turned to walk inside, her brown leather sandals making gentle plopping noises on the rock sidewalk.

As I walked to my car, I saw Jerry driving in the parking lot. He parked next to me, lowered his window and said, "We could have come together. I want to talk to you later about Esther Cooper. Found out some interesting things about her."

"I didn't know that you had the same idea as I did. Maybe she'll tell you different stuff," I said, referring to the lady inside Tranquility House. "You being the law and all."

"Fat chance," he said. "I'll probably get less." Still, he might ask her questions I hadn't thought of.

"We'll talk at two o'clock," Jerry said, getting out of his cruiser and walking toward the building.

From a pay phone, I called Peter's answering machine, leaving a message: "When you talk to the lady at the shelter, ask if Linda Pavell ever came with Beth, or been there. Find out what you can, and run Linda Pavell's name through your computer, please. Pavell. One v, two ll's. And one more thing, please check and see if any baby boys disappeared around the time of Charles's adoption—about twenty-eight years or so, give or take six months—from St. Augustine, Florida."

I stopped at a diner and ate a greasy hamburger loaded with mayonnaise, then headed toward Rushing River Junction.

I was supposed to meet Jerry at two o'clock at Oldman's, so I decided to go there and sit outside, even though I was a little early. The place was quiet. I'd go so far as to say lonely. No livestock, no chickens, no dogs, no cats. No barn. No horses, no mules, no garden at Oldman's house.

I sat on the front stoop, thinking.

Chapter Nineteen

I had an idea. There should be a Web site or some national registry that anyone who felt that he or she was stolen by Simpson-Getts could have their DNA tested and parents who had a child stolen could register their DNA. All three sets of DNA's could be stored in a computer, and matched up.

That way, even if the parents died, the stolen person could still find out who his birth family was. I'd have to speak to Peter about this and see if I could get this going as a national resource, after the murders were solved— www.stolenbaby.com., or simpson-getts.com or something like that. Get donations to pay for DNA tests if the people couldn't afford it.

How was Esther involved in all this? She had felt free to walk right inside Oldman's house because the door was open. She didn't just knock, leave the eggs, and leave.

Could she have been the one who broke into my house and left the threatening note? But why? What in blazes could she want that she thought was in papers at my house? Was she worried about who might buy the property next to hers if Oldman's property was put on the market? Did she think I'd approve the sale of it to developers?

Why was Oldman's house so small if they were rich? Maybe Oldman and Jessica were not intending to stay here; just use this place to lay low for a while after the illegal adoptions. You can't just appear with a toddler or two without explanations. Here, at the time, they'd probably didn't have any neighbors. And if you move somewhere new, you don't have to explain your family to them.

And then Jessica had died. Oldman had stayed on here, then, maybe because she hadn't left him any money. Cut from the will. Was he being punished, financially, because he had fought her about the illegal adoptions?

Probably. From what I'd heard about the personality of Jessica Shaw Reilly; that sounded highly likely.

Jerry drove up, parked, and I walked over to his cruiser. He handed me booties and gloves, and we walked over and he unlocked the door. We put on our booties and gloves.

"These are the keys to everything in the house and to Oldman's truck," he told me. "I want to talk to you about Tranquility House and about Esther Cooper, but let's get this other thing over with first," he said. We went inside. "Do you think Charles—and Beth, if we find her—want anything from this old place?" he said, looking at the furniture. "What do you do in a case like that?" he said. "If they don't want anything from the house. Or if one wants things from the house and the other doesn't."

"Estimate its value and use that as part of the inventory

list so that the other beneficiary gets the equal value amount of money for it," I said, following him down the hall.

"I never knew it was so complicated after a death," he said. We reached the desk in the back bedroom, and he unlocked it. The front of the big oak desk opened down to create a wooden surface to write on. Jerry pulled up a chair and motioned for me to sit at the desk.

I began looking through the papers. There was a copy of the will. That was a relief. I wouldn't have to go through getting a court order to get it. It was straight-forward; Beth and Charles equal beneficiaries.

Right of first refusal on the property to me, and my right to approve whomever was purchasing the property, except if either Beth or Charles wanted to buy it—one from the other. If they did, the price was to be settled on by getting three appraisals from local Realtors, and taking the average as the sales price.

No photographs. A small insurance policy in each of the two children's names. Twenty thousand each. Paid up in full. No veteran's papers. A paper from the bank saying that the mortgage was satisfied and the house was his free and clear. Ditto with his truck title. No payments due on anything. Income tax papers seemed to be in order and up-to-date. Three old saving bonds. Two bank books. Certificate of Baptism for Oldman.

While I looked, I talked in spurts to Jerry, telling him about what Miss Paternoster had said at Tranquility House.

She said the same things to Jerry. Beth had done well while on her medicine.

He'd pressed her for details about Beth's relationship. It was an unhealthy domination of one person by another. She said Beth tended to be very insecure and timid; a follower.

Linda was a "dominant personality type." There was some rumors of Linda having a "nasty boyfriend."

I made mental notes on what needed to be done. I put everything back where I'd found it. I closed up the desk and Jerry relocked it.

"Did you find an address book anywhere?" I asked Jerry.

"No, come to think of it, I didn't," Jerry said.

"The only phone is in the living room," I said. It was a real old, black rotary dial phone. "It seems logical that it would be there, next to it."

"We checked this house with a fine-tooth comb, as they used to say," he said. "No address book."

"That's funny," I said.

"Consider it missing, then," Jerry said.

"You can call Charles at rehab and ask," I said.

He scratched his head. "I hate callin' that kid," Jerry said. "But I guess I'll have to. Is the phone shut off yet?"

"No."

"Mind if I use it? It will go on Oldman's bill."

"I don't mind, and I don't think Oldman will, either."

"Ghoulish sense of humor you got there, Ranger. Kids ever tease you about your name?"

"John? Sure. A name for a toilet in some areas."

"No, stupid, I mean Ranger—you know, like the Lone Ranger."

"No. Two things stopped them, I guess. One was if they teased me, I didn't know what the heck they were talking about, and not getting any rise out of me, they stopped. Because, to tell the truth, I was a dumb kid and thought the word was *Long* Ranger—like he was tall, or that he ranged a long way."

"Boy, you *were* dumb! What was the second thing?"

"That I would beat the doo-doo out of them if they tried teasing me. I got big early."

"Is that a warning?"

"Would I threaten a cop?" I asked jokingly.

"Not and live."

"Case closed."

"You know, I really, really hate arguing with lawyers," he said with an amused smirk as he left to go down the hall to the phone. "Wait here," he said, as he left.

Jerry returned with a look on his face that told me all I needed to know. He'd gotten through to Charles: "Near the phone. A small brown book."

"Did you get a copy of Oldman's phone bill for the month before he died?" I asked.

"Four months. Not *one* long distance."

I thought of my own. I groaned.

I was glad that I was through with my first scan of the papers. The sooner I could get done with my work as executor, the sooner I'd be happy. But it didn't look too bad. Oldman's legal affairs were in better order than I had hoped. I had enough information to do what was immediately necessary.

"Did Finley have a safe deposit box?" I asked.

"He did, and I'm working on getting access to it."

"That takes time, usually." I said. I told Jerry about Charles's memories of what might be St. Augustine. "Getting a sample of his DNA might be a good idea," he said.

We walked back through the house and outside. Jerry said, "Esther Cooper spent twelve years in prison when she was a lot younger. She and her husband robbed a grocery store in Ohio. Her maiden name was Cooper. She took her maiden name back after the divorce. Her married name was

Campbell. She insisted that Campbell forced her to partici-
pate in the robbery–murder. It appears she's been clean
since she got out of prison. Her husband is in prison with
no possibility of getting out anytime soon," Jerry said.
"And the preliminary blood tests indicate that it is her own
blood on the sweater. She's O negative. Oldman's O positive. I went to see her again early this morning. She has a
history of self-mutilation. On her arms. Seeing Oldman's
body upset her and triggered a relapse. I told her to go talk
to Alice. Alice will be able to get her into a free self-help
group."

"I've never been able to understand self-mutilation," I
said. It was ironic that I'd thought of self-mutilation in
regard to Beth, and it turned out that it was my own egg
lady who did it. Life can be odd. We walked to our vehicles.

Jerry opened his car door. "Neither do I. Thank God it's
rare. She said it helps her ease the pain."

I felt sad that people feel they need to do that. I followed
Jerry's cruiser out to the main road.

So. Was Esther still a suspect? Maybe.

Chapter Twenty

Jerry called early the next morning. "Guess what's in the safety deposit box?"

I couldn't guess. The phone had rung just as I was shaving. I was in a bad mood.

"Blackmail. Blackmail notes written in block letters, like the one you got. Someone was blackmailing Finley about stealing from the estate. There was a lot of money in there, too. Stacks of it. Which I suspect might belong to Jessica's estate, and other people's, too. He was skimming money from clients. The bank manager, who's good at financial stuff, says that's what it looks like to him.

"And you were right; he was getting ready to book. Passport was in there. Plane ticket. Ironically, for today. He was about to take off for South America. The bank manager is helping count the money. It'll take a while. Talk to you later." The line went dead.

One more crooked lawyer. Great. I went back to the bathroom and finished shaving.

The phone rang near noon. I was making myself a tuna-fish sandwich on rye bread.

Peter said, "Hi. I went to see Esmeralda. Nice, but strange. She said she had some kind of spiritual awakening—rebirth—a few years ago and changed her name from Barbara Cohen to Esmeralda. She calls it her 'Anti-Contumacious Resurrection and Renewal.' "

"What the hell is that?"

"Contumacious—I looked it up—is 'inclined toward rebellion; apt to oppose authority.' "

"So she no longer rebels against authority, in other words now?"

"Right. Perpetual humility," Peter said.

"So, she founded Our Lady of Perpetual Humility?"

"Right. That's her," Peter said.

"Humble now, not rebellious. How humble are you, when you name a whole church after yourself?"

"We didn't discuss that," Peter said.

"What did she say about Beth?"

"Same as what she wrote. Hasn't seen Beth lately. Did hear rumors of Beth getting into trouble. Never saw Linda Pavell; said Linda had a creepy boyfriend Beth mentioned sometimes. His name was Wayne Grundek. Esmeralda said Beth cried a lot, got upset easily. Depressed. Didn't seem to know what to do with her life. That's all she knows."

"Did you get my message about St. Augustine? Can you find out if any babies disappeared in St. Augustine, Florida about the time Charles's adoption? Somewhere in your papers you have the dates from when we were trying to locate Beth."

"I do have them somewhere," he said. "Gee, I almost forgot. Esmeralda said since she wrote you she heard a friend of Beth's was coming into money and they were going to open up something called 'Angels Watching' or maybe it was 'Watching Angels;' she couldn't remember. Esmeralda dismissed it as wishful thinking."

"Thanks, Peter," I said, and hung up.

The phone rang; it was Jerry. "I'm in my office if you need me," he said. I told him about Esmeralda. Snorted when I told him about the Contumacious part.

"Do you think Beth could have been the blackmailer and wrote that threatening note to you?"

"Nothing would surprise me," I said.

"But it was her own money, anyway."

"Which Finley obviously wasn't giving her like he was supposed to, to take care of her," I said.

"But she had run away, with the woman," he said.

"True. Maybe George didn't know where she was," I said. "That was my impression when I saw him. He was covering up that he had 'lost track' of her. He *was* responsible for her financially, and he wasn't doing it."

"Probably didn't try very hard to find her—he'd have had to give her money to live on," Jerry said. "The files that are missing. Do you think she stole them as proof of his thievery, in case she got caught in the blackmail scheme?"

"It was her own money and she wasn't getting it."

"You mean that she felt she was entitled to help and she wasn't getting it?" Jerry asked.

"Makes sense, if you think about it that way."

"She was desperate for money," he said.

"The flaw in our theory is that the other woman was

supposed to be coming into money, according to Esmeralda. And Beth, according to a couple of people, was depressed and a follower, not a leader."

We both thought of it at the same time: Linda Pavell.

"Do you think it was Linda, the other patient from Tranquility House who was the blackmailer?" I asked.

Jerry said sharply, "Who told you she was a patient? She was an *employee,* not a patient!"

I thought over Miss Paternoster's carefully worded sentences. She hadn't actually said, but I'd gotten the impression that she was a fellow patient, and "worse" than Beth.

"Well," Jerry said, annoyed and defensive. "I have copies of her employment records from Tranquility House. They're right in front of me."

"I believe you, Jerry," I said. "I misunderstood her."

If Jerry was a woman, this argument would be like the first-time-I-had-let-her-down argument. I wanted to laugh; I must have made noises.

"What's so darn funny?"

"Nothing. I was just thinking of something else."

"Well, I'm not laughing," he said.

I called Faith Christine. I told her that I had goofed in not asking Miss Paternoster specifically if Linda was a patient or an employee. I missed her, so I told her that I needed to come over and tell her about Esmeralda in person.

Chapter Twenty-one

I t was Faith Christine who jarred my memory. "Didn't Mrs. Webster talk to you about 'angels watching' the day of the funeral?" she said.

I searched my memory. She didn't talk to me, but I overheard something when I was sitting on the porch. I heard something through the window. It was about those Guardian Angel pins, wasn't it? Or was it? What was it she said? Something to the effect "It was weird and I didn't like it one bit."

"I need to talk to Mrs. Webster," I said. "Would you call and ask if we can come over?"

"Sure," Faith Christine said.

Mrs. Webster met us at the door, pleased to have company. We sat in her pink, white, and green living room.

She went everywhere with the Senior Citizens group; bus tours which offered big discounts. One tour had stopped overnight at a place that was "a disgrace," she said. "It was run by two strange women," Mrs. Webster said. "It was weird, I can tell you that. Kind of like in that movie *Psycho*—like the Bates Motel. Two ladies ran it. Our group said that we'll never go back there again. Angels all over the place—which ordinarily, I wouldn't have minded, but this was weird. They were hand-painted on the walls of the bedrooms, and they were grotesque. They looked like witches. We couldn't wait to get out of there."

"Where was this place?" I asked.

"Down near Monterey," she said. "Beautiful country."

"Would you remember the name of the ladies that ran the place?" Faith Christine asked.

"The bossy one was Linda, a Linda something, I think. Stringy black hair, kind of big nose. I couldn't tell you the other person's name. Quiet as a mouse, she was, and I would say she was under the other woman's thumb. The lady who runs the tours, says The Angel Watching Motel is off our list of approved places to stay."

We left, after thanking them.

"I'll get the address from Information," Faith Christine said. She called Information and got the address and phone number of the motel. She got it a sneaky way by asking the operator if the Angel Watching Motel was on Monterey Boulevard (she made that up), and the information operator said no, it was on Oleander. 1362 Oleander.

We called Jerry. After that, things moved fast.

We were outside of 1362 Oleander at three o'clock the next afternoon, just down the street, looking the place over. My truck was around the corner.

The Angel Watching Motel was run-down, decrepit, and

probably bug-infested. Weeds growing up through the side-walk, trash all over the front sidewalk. It was a dump.

Both Peter and Jerry's computers had come back yester-day with the information that Linda Pavell, Pavel, Pavvel, Smith, etc., was one bad lady. There were outstanding war-rants for her arrest. She had a history of violence and of using vulnerable, weak people. Preyed on elderly men a lot; flattered them, romanced them, took their money, and then left them destitute. She charmed people, then gradually took over their lives and finances.

At fifteen, she'd stabbed her mother to death in Pitts-burgh. She'd spent years in and out of correctional and psychiatric facilities in Pennsylvania.

She knew the system, and had learned how to beat it. She paid people to provide fake references (fifty bucks a time) and she had beat the system of checking for felonies and arrests by name changes. She was thirty-eight now. She avoided places where they used fingerprints for background checks. She worked in out-of-the way places where she would be less likely to be found out. She only needed to work there long enough to select a wealthy victim. In Beth's case, the money had been harder to get at, but gossip told her there was a lot of it to be had.

Usually she was able to set up housekeeping with her victim as she pretended to be their best friend and protector. In the case of Beth, she had a more complex long-range plan. Obviously, she used the blackmail money for the down payment on this motel. Planning for her old age.

"She's becoming more and more sinister," Jerry said.

Faith Christine added, "Lord, Jerry, how could that be when you start out by killing your mother? How much worse can you get than that?"

Chapter Twenty-two

"I'm going in," Faith Christine insisted. "Beth knows me, at least a little, and maybe I can talk her out peacefully," she said, as she and I sat with Jerry and Ken in his police cruiser parked down the street. My truck was parked just behind it.

Monterey cops were there, too, in unmarked cars and one police cruiser, out of sight of the motel.

"You can't stop me, Jerry, either. I'm going in there as a citizen inquiring about a room," she said facetiously.

"Wait," I said. "I'm coming with you."

"Wait, we'll all go together," Jerry said. "I don't want anything to happen to Beth if I can help it. She's been through enough, and I don't think much of this is her fault. I think she's been victimized enough in her life already. Maybe you two can help get her out safely."

He got out of the cruiser and went to talk to the Monterey

177

police. They had been surprisingly laid-back, figuring that cops had had enough bad publicity lately, and were allowing Jerry to handle it more than they would have normally; cops are very territorial creatures as a rule.

It didn't hurt that Jerry had a cousin on the force in Monterey. The club. In a sense, Jerry was a member of the club here. The police family. Now that I thought about it, getting along with people was one of Jerry's best policing skills.

Faith Christine had slid out of the car quietly as we waited. She was on the sidewalk and was sneaking sideways, closer and closer to the door of the motel office, by the time Jerry started back toward us. Quickly, I got out and stood next to her. I stood on the side toward the motel so as to block her. I wanted her to wait for Jerry. She did, barely.

Jerry motioned for Ken to stay in the cruiser, and he did. Jerry had on street clothes, not his uniform, although he had his badge, I was sure, handy and ready to show.

We walked in and we were lucky. They were both behind the counter, and Linda looked happy that three potential customers had walked in.

From the looks of the place; they didn't have many. And probably no return business. Beth took a few seconds before she recognized Faith Christine, and she looked happy and relieved, then her facial expression changed to worry. Worry for herself, Faith Christine, or discovery? I didn't know which.

Her demeanor was one of total defeat and unhappiness. Her eyes were red-rimmed. I took that to indicate that she was not happy with her life. And that she wasn't getting medication. I was surprised that she had red hair. No one had mentioned that. She had dark circles under her eyes.

But did she know Oldman was dead?

Her hair looked unwashed and disheveled. She looked ungroomed and uncared for, her white T-shirt dirty.

Linda, was by contrast, one tough-looking cookie. Obviously, the Boss. I could see her cast in a women's prison movie as the sadistic matron.

The thought passed through my mind that she was the type who would have saved the knife somewhere, considering it a lucky omen, because she had gotten away with murder—twice, she thought. Linda Pavell killed. Maybe many, many more times than we knew. Maybe a serial killer.

Fingerprints, maybe, were the key. Fingerprints in Oldman's house. One of the unidentified prints they'd found. Hers? And maybe some from that man Wayne Grundek?

Oldman had had tea with her. He'd made tea for someone that he'd thought had come to discuss Beth and what was best for her. He would have been relieved, because Beth had been gone for two years; and here was a lady who knew where she was and said she was "taking care of her."

Well, she had taken care of him, all right. And the next day, she "took care" of George Finley, who she was blackmailing about stealing Beth's money from the estate. If she'd known about the illegal adoptions, she could have been blackmailing both men about that.

She'd probably gone to George Finley's originally to find out how much Beth was worth, found out what he was doing—or not doing—and began blackmailing him. She probably hadn't found out about the illegal adoptions until *after* she'd killed George Finley and stolen the Shaw files.

By then it was too late. She must have been furious when she found out she had missed a golden opportunity.

I thought of Finley saying, "Not one more." Dollar, probably. And she needed more money, obviously, to fix up the motel.

She had probably come first to get money out of Oldman, and when that didn't work out, she got mad. Not angry; mad. Mad as in crazy. And I had to admit she looked formidable. I could easily picture Wayne Grundek waiting outside and maybe coming in to help if he was needed. If he hadn't wiped the Budweiser beer bottle clean, it might have his fingerprints on it. He was probably outside, drinking the beer, while she was in the house having tea and trying to get what she wanted out of Oldman Reilly.

And a few days later, searching my house for whatever information she thought I had, and leaving the threatening note. Before things had turned nasty, had Oldman mentioned to her that I was going to be the executor of his will? Was that why my house was searched? Or had she found that out when she stole the files from George Finley's office? George Finley had drawn up the papers making me the executor, as Oldman's lawyer.

It was an evil woman we were facing. But Linda Pavell, as evil as she was, was no match for Faith Christine when she was riled up. I could see Faith Christine had sized up the situation. Maybe thinking the same things I was thinking.

"You get out here, right now, Beth Reilly. You come over here to me," she said so suddenly that Linda didn't have time to react. Beth scurried like a mouse out around the counter and ran into Faith Christine's arms. They were gone, out the door, before Linda could react.

Jerry moved quickly, and he went around and brought Linda Pavell out from behind the counter before she quite comprehended what was going on. First she'd thought we were customers; then she thought we were Beth's friends until Jerry brought out his badge and handcuffs.

Linda had a long list of outstanding warrants for her arrest, and she knew it. Jerry read her her rights as he snapped cuffs on. Outside, she was put into a Monterey police car. They arrested Wayne Grundek out in the back alleyway, where he was emptying garbage.

We went to the Monterey Police station. Faith Christine and I drove there in my truck; Ken drove Jerry.

They were considering adding a kidnapping charge as Beth said she had been held against her will for two months. Beth hadn't known Oldman was dead, but she implicated Linda in both murders. Linda had been gone from the motel when both murders occurred and during the time of the break-in at my house. Beth had seen bloody clothing on Linda on both days the murders occurred.

It was in the hands of the police now. Hopefully, they had enough evidence from both crime scenes to convict Linda and Wayne, if it turned out that he had taken part in the murders. He was eager to talk. Linda had some files in their room at the motel that "looked all legal-like," he said. One of the folders had blood spots on it. Oldman's address book and other incriminating items were at the motel, and he had seen Linda writing notes in block lettering, he said.

"Thank God," I said to Faith Christine, as we got back in my truck hours and hours later. I meant that this whole thing was over. I breathed a sigh of relief. Beth had not been at either crime scene. Beth had said that she thought she knew where a big knife was hidden in Linda's room under a mattress.

After she gave her statement, Beth had been taken to the hospital to get evaluated. She seemed to be in shock from the news about her father, and Linda's involvement in it.

"Well, it wasn't the miners after us, after all," I said. "And I've been thinking I might begin helping again with the high school rodeo. Right after I help Charles—and Beth, if she wants to—try to find their birth parents. I have a feeling that Charles is going to be all right from now on."

"They've missed you at the rodeo," Faith Christine said as we drove off. "It would be nice if you went back to helping again."

She was quiet as we drove up to the next stoplight, then she added, "I just hope that there'll be money to set Beth up in one of those small group homes you mentioned. Jerry said that he thought some of the money in the safe deposit box belonged to Jessica's estate. He thinks that the Shaw estate has more money than George Finley let on."

"I think Beth might be charged with a few things," I said. "That money might be all used up paying for lawyers getting Beth out of this mess," I said.

"No, it won't," Faith Christine said in a very forceful, positive way. "I know a very good lawyer, who knows a lot about this case, whose law degree is still good in this state," she said, as she settled onto the seat. "And he's going to work on this one for free. Make sure everything comes out all right."

I groaned.